THE
WRITING
IN THE
STONE

THE
WRITING
IN THE
STONE

IRVING FINKEL

illustrated by Angharad Crossley

Medina Publishing

The Writing in the Stone

published by
Medina Publishing Ltd
310 Ewell Road
Surbiton
Surrey KT6 7AL
www.medinapublishing.com

© Irving Finkel 2018
Illustrations Angharad Crossley 2018

We acknowledge with gratitude the photographs taken specially for this work by
Nils Makrow, Mathilde Touillon-Ricci and Shahrokh Razmjou.

ISBN 978-1-911487-20-3 trade hardback
ISBN: 978-1-911487-06-7 trade paperback

British Library Cataloguing-in-Publication Data:
A catalogue record for this publication is available from the British Library

Printed and bound by Toppan Leefung Printers, China

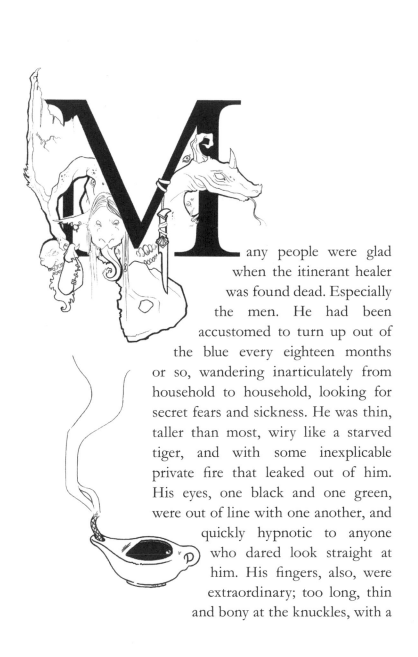

any people were glad when the itinerant healer was found dead. Especially the men. He had been accustomed to turn up out of the blue every eighteen months or so, wandering inarticulately from household to household, looking for secret fears and sickness. He was thin, taller than most, wiry like a starved tiger, and with some inexplicable private fire that leaked out of him. His eyes, one black and one green, were out of line with one another, and quickly hypnotic to anyone who dared look straight at him. His fingers, also, were extraordinary; too long, thin and bony at the knuckles, with a single, worn silver ring with Egyptian writing, and blue tattoos on the back of his hands. Blackened strips of animal hide, knotted and re-knotted, gripped his left wrist like a manacle.

The men hated him, and muttered together. The healer performed wonders with the women, who returned with shining eyes from a consultation, clutching a bag of amuletic herbs or a twist of wool, confident of recovery or a pregnancy to come.

The body was found by two writer-boys in the early morning, running in the mist with a dog before the heat and the demands of the school curriculum. The dead healer was lying awkwardly down by a small branch canal remote across the fields, smeared from writhing on the mud; cold now and stiff. His feet were scarred and bruised, the blued hands pressed on the belly as if to stifle pain. The boys looked once, carefully, and ran.

The mayor, lazy and overweight, sent two men with a donkey cart to collect the body. The word had gone round like lightning. Many people followed them out along the canal and watched with a complex mix of emotions as the long, angular puppet in its grimy dressing gown was manhandled onto the worn matting. A swelling moan of lament gathered as the cart made its bumpy way across the hard ground towards the white glare of the town, the body slithering in its ropes and seemingly stirring from sleep. The ragged troupe of mourners stood back as the cart, parked by the outer wall of the mayor's house, was relieved of its burden, and they stayed there for much of the morning, talking, lamenting and, in some cases, even weeping.

The mayor ordered all the accoutrements removed and the body washed for the morrow. The operation was carried out ungrudgingly by the two old women who usually performed the task. The healer was known to be malodorous, and his long matted hair would defy any ministrations, but both were curious to inspect him under his robes. There had been many stories about him. A pouch of slimy leather at the waist was tied in a dense tangle of knots. The midwife sliced through the cord with the healer's own knife; the knots would need to be carefully burned. Her assistant laid the slimy membrane carefully to one side, together with his leather shoulder bag; there was no question of opening either.

The crones sat by him in the closed room, immobile, with a single oil-lamp between them, bent low through the night. The very shadows cast by the angular limbs would have frightened most watchers, but the two old women had seen all the visions before, and both carried death-amulets and safety herbs hidden under their own garments. They were undisturbed, therefore, even unaware, when the healer's demons arrived, straining from outside to see through the irregular slats across the opening, green eyes gleaming to confirm him dead. He had alternately bullied and cajoled them with his magic, banishing them dismissively when they overstepped, but sometimes summoning them for conversation, or to recruit their night-shaded services. Their scratching, leathery wings or eagles' feet brushed at the outside walls as they sighed and circled; rivals or enemies from the darkness were united in recognition of his faded skill. Some stayed on at the corners of the hut, dark sentinels against some unimaginable foe, folded down like dormant bats, but watching, flicking their tongues and hooding their eyes until the first hint of the sun discomposed them and they vanished.

After they had detached certain mementoes to pass on to barren women, the midwives wrapped the body. In the new morning light he lay rigid and inert; a plain rough cloth tied round with rope and he was readied. One of the women washed down the death table with a river pebble and salt water. The dead man's possessions were straight-jacketed severely in a new cloth, and later handed, with the knife, to the mayor.

The mayor inspected the knife apprehensively without touching it. It was well finished, with a decorated handle and a strange, thin blade; it resembled no local work with which he was familiar. Corpse and blade alike had made the house unclean, but he would have to call the priest later anyway. He prodded the pouch and the bag guardedly with the tip of one finger. Perhaps the whole lot should be burned. Or perhaps he should make a list of the contents with the priest; he was quite unsure what the repellent things might contain. He pushed them aside and stepped outside into the parched garden to stand under the straggled awning. There had been an unexplained death within his jurisdiction, and something would need to be done to show that he had tried to bring the circumstances into the open. The odd dead body out in the country was all very well, and the magician was not at all the first unexplained and unnatural death within living memory, but they were not so far off the beaten track here, and he would need to proceed carefully. Some officious tax inspector, drinking with the farmers, might get wind of it and loose talk in the capital was often troublesome in its consequences.

They brought in the priest and his assistant as the mayor was eating some bread with little river-fish and olives. He invited them to join him. The younger priest helped himself but his colleague contented himself with a couple of dates and some water.

"He is well known to us, this wanderer," remarked the priest. "A thorn in our side, if you like. He had power wherever he went; it is true, with his recipes and spells. He could under-cut us when he wanted. When he was here, all the sick went to him."

"So, you are pleased, then?" asked the mayor, chewing. "Good for business, we might say?"

The priest made a deprecating movement with his hand.

"Possibly. But this is not of our doing. The gods are always in the temple. The people always come back."

"Did he have his own gods?"

"Surely. He picked up names and magic wherever he went. I conversed with him once or twice. He had been east, far over the mountains, and knew healers here, there and everywhere. He spoke several of those highland languages. The man was a renegade. They schooled him as a healer like all of us, somewhere in the south; he went through the whole process, like me. Learning the signs. Writing tablets. Copying out the classics. He was a gifted reader, apparently, with a remarkable memory. But there were problems with him, they said. He liked to experiment and wouldn't do what he was told, so they threw him out."

"Experiment?" said the mayor.

"With incantation work. He was obsessed with the demons. Always wanted to see them, when he drove them out of people, instead of turning his back. He was not afraid of them at all. People said he sometimes used the spells to make them come, not go away. That, of course, was utterly forbidden. And ghosts used to follow him. When he was brought in to banish them, they would stay with him instead, like a pack of hunting dogs. People say that when he walked at night there was always a shining crowd following him, people who should be in the city of the dead."

The mayor swallowed convulsively. This was not the sort of thing he wanted to hear at all. Thank the gods this monster was dead.

"What happens now?"

"When we bury him we must use strong means to keep him there. There are ancient words… I shall look them up later. Let us hope that he will be happy down there and not make mischief for us now he is one of them himself."

The mayor nodded. He was truly frightened. There could be general panic if all the ghosts decided to invade at once. Like an army, marching at nightfall. It was all too easy to imagine it. He gazed vacantly at the priest.

"Must we bury him here? He is not from this place, after all."

But even as he spoke he knew it was nonsense. The cursed, trouble-making body must be put in the ground without delay.

* * *

The burial was underway. Alone with the body, the two priests had sealed the eyes, ears, mouth and nostrils, the older articulating certain ancient, hissing words with extra care. When they were finally done the mayor's henchmen – not without violence – managed to stuff the scarecrow body into a large terracotta jar. Wet goatskin was then stretched across the mouth and, as it dried, tied around with seven knots, the tying of which was known only to the older priest. Fresh river clay was then wrapped around the whole, sealed and re-sealed with another powerful amulet. The healer was ready for his last journey.

The procession, the reverse of that of the previous day, made its laborious way out of the gate towards the cemetery. The mayor had forbidden anyone to accompany the party, but a few determined stragglers followed from a distance.

The great jar was to be buried deep. After the priests had laid their figurines and other secret deposits in place they squatted in silence. Then, hands upraised to the beating sun, they pronounced in an ageless, fluting cadence the final solemn oath to ensure that the body would rest in the earth untroubled. Walking backwards away from the grave, they made way for the sexton so that the jar could be covered, densely packed down and deep against the jackals that were always on the lookout for a new arrival. There would be no kind of memorial above the ground, no inscription or stone work. Those who might need to know where he was would do so.

Having purified themselves in the outer entrance, the three men were drinking wine together. The older priest sighed and tipped out the contents of the magician's bag onto the table. This revealed:

A cluster of mixed herbs tied together in a clump;

A small alabaster bottle with the neck sealed;

A flint blade;

Several carved or twisted beads — one of brilliant blue;

A piece of amber;

A dead, dried frog;

Two dead, small scorpions;

Some heavy balls of greasy black stone;

A jagged star-shaped piece of un-worked rock crystal;

A skin containing snake scales;

A bronze pin;

A flat slither of painted red clay inscribed with small foreign letters;

Four cylinders of stone carved with symbols, bored through;

A grimy necklace with small, dull stones;

A strip of animal skin with black designs;

The shell of a large, winged beetle.

"What is all this stuff?" said the mayor testily. "It's more for your hands than mine, I tell you."

The priest nodded gravely and scooped the material carefully back into the bag. He picked it up together with the pouch. This was unexpectedly heavy and he had already decided that he must examine its contents in privacy.

"We have work to do. Recitations and purifications. I shall send something for the house with my assistant. Fumigants, of course, and a text to be hung up. If you see or hear anything, I shall be at the temple."

The priests left.

Making some excuse the older priest rid himself of his colleague's presence and stepped across the courtyard to the long low room at the far corner where he would not be disturbed. It was obvious that the dead individual had commanded powerful and obscure forces and he slit open the pouch fearfully.

There were carved fragments of lapis lazuli and twisted gold whose purpose was unclear and a tiny ivory statuette of a goddess. He looked down thoughtfully at the unidentifiable little figure. He would put her before the Statue as a votive. An anonymous gift. That way, the goddess from afar would be under My Lady's observation and could get up to no harm.

Finally, his fingers turned over a curious, plump, pale-yellow pebble, one end a bulbous nose pierced through at the base like the lug on a jar, the other end cracked flat open, revealing a complex design etched in the broken surface. It was a tumble of ancient signs that he knew from the clay – embedded in the hardness; surely an amulet of timeless and unimaginable power.

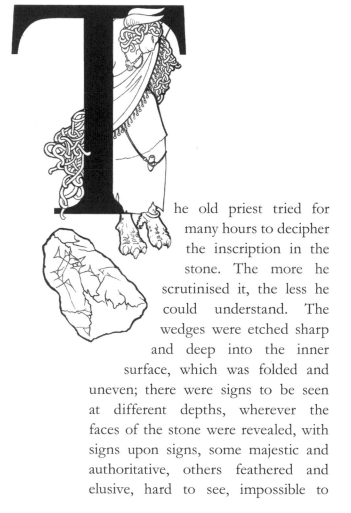

he old priest tried for many hours to decipher the inscription in the stone. The more he scrutinised it, the less he could understand. The wedges were etched sharp and deep into the inner surface, which was folded and uneven; there were signs to be seen at different depths, wherever the faces of the stone were revealed, with signs upon signs, some majestic and authoritative, others feathered and elusive, hard to see, impossible to count. The inscription before him was like no other he had ever encountered.

He could make out one or two signs, those for "god" and for "right", which seemed to confirm that it was a divine communication. Beyond that, he could read nothing. There were endless combinations that he just did not recognise. Nothing like them had found a place in the traditional lists he'd had to memorise as a boy. Since the traditional script was so ancient and so fruitful it was always possible to encounter an unfamiliar sign over which heads had to be scratched. His own teacher had once encouraged his harassed pupils by declaring that no man since the Sages had ever mastered all the signs, every one. Not even, he had added, the distant scholars in the Academy at Babylon who, famous for their learning, were even able to explain the inscriptions written before the Flood that workmen sometimes found when digging deep foundations. In times of long peace there were scribal competitions, and the most learned scribes always delighted in discovering hidden writings or inventing new possibilities, but the signs in the stone were not in that sort of tradition at all. Sometimes, of course, it was possible to guess at the meaning of an unknown sign, but here were signs in abundance that were entirely alien. Not only could he not recognise them, he was uncertain where one sign stopped and the next began.

The partly-rounded pebble must have had some wholly remote origin. Only the gods could write in stone, reflected the priest. They could write on clay, or in flesh or on stone. It was all one to them. If they had a message, there was always a medium. No human artisan ever weaved those signs into living stone. It must have been a god... But if a god had written it, how much more imperative now was the need to read it? The message must be of incalculable importance. An answer, perhaps, to all those prayers, the longed-for oracles and despairing appeals that wafted skywards throughout the day from shrines and temples all over the country. Perhaps one god, moved to reply, had taken his stylus and flowing molten stone – like bronze in a crucible – written the message and tossed it to earth. There it must have lain, a fallen shooting star, cooling into hardness, awaiting the most learned scribe in the kingdom to decipher the script and pass on the message. By fate or destiny it had come into the hands of that mystic, dangerous creature who, through his own violent death, had been used by the gods to deliver the stone to him. That, then, was the reason for his dying here. *To bring the message.*

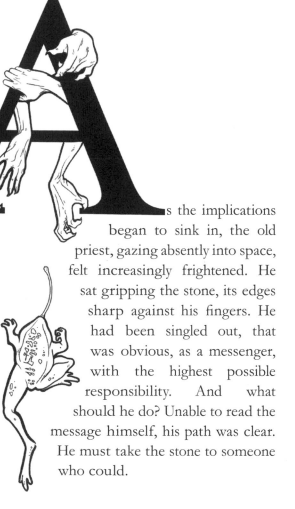

s the implications began to sink in, the old priest, gazing absently into space, felt increasingly frightened. He sat gripping the stone, its edges sharp against his fingers. He had been singled out, that was obvious, as a messenger, with the highest possible responsibility. And what should he do? Unable to read the message himself, his path was clear. He must take the stone to someone who could.

The priest wrapped the stone in an old piece of linen and hid it carefully in his chamber.

Overnight, there was an attack on the homesteads of the town. Demons galore were on the warpath, invading quiet people's houses, sliding greasily through the gaps in the doorjambs or in by the windows, disturbing slumbering families and tormenting babies with their noxious breath and hooked nails. Long-dead relatives appeared, evanescent and beyond reach, their hollowed fingers pointing or beckoning, empty eyes agape. The rich saw the worst ones, vast and green lizard men, winged and with swollen bellies, long webbed fingers and jaws dripping gall.

No one slept. Screams and stifled cries came from many households; several citizens died, two went mad and one disappeared for good. An army of resentful beings, usually mild-mannered and generally invisible, wreaked their mourning rage on the defenceless. Their traffic with mankind henceforth would be barred; there would be no further subtle calls across the abyss, his compelling, whispered spells now silenced forever. And they resented it like spoiled human children. The pickings, the heat of a fire, the lure of communal singing, the sweetness of a child's pure limbs were to be snatched from them, condemned again to their subterranean, ill-lit limbo, with only the murmur of their neighbours' wings and the remote whistling of certain divine superintendents to distract their frantic minds from the horizon of dust.

No one went for the priests. No person would leave his house. Bedding-buried heads and blocked ears were their only defence as the ageless, reptilian beings swirled above their rooftops, or strutted gangster-like down the streets, bent on mischief and mayhem and revenge.

The mayor alone came to the temple, wide-eyed through the pandemonium outside. There were ominous bundles lying on the street, hard to make out in the darkness, and other threatening shapes and perturbing noises. Leaving his wives, he ran with his head down, heart crashing unevenly in his chest, stark fear from childhood ungovernable in his soul. He found the priest with his assistant before the image, immobile and silent, his eyes fixed on the inlaid eyes above them. The mayor stood behind them, taut against the wall, his hands over his eyes. He thought he might die at any minute.

The priest spent the last watch of the night closeted in silence, contemplative and anxious. He would leave at dawn, he decided. It was treacherous, perhaps, to abandon his young colleague under such circumstances, but the trouble would be finished now. The weight of the stone and its message, meanwhile, was insupportable. He wanted to look for an omen, something in the temple incense patterns, a sign in the stars, or a chance toad in his sandal. Better still would be to solicit a message from a sheep's liver, with careful questions to pin down the suitable day, the propitious moment. But there was no time for any of that now, nor could he explain his behaviour to anyone. He would be up and gone before dawn. His colleague, rising betimes himself for the early prayer, would assume he was still asleep; it did not always require both of them to welcome the sun as if the daily breaking-through were each time a triumph. The sun, he considered, would rise anyway.

He would carry the bare minimum, for his shaven head, unassuming clothing and non-calloused hands would proclaim him to be a priest on the move, and everyone knew that priestly wealth stayed in the temples. The question was, where should he go? The obvious answer was Nineveh itself, where today the greatest scholars lived and where the king himself was rumoured to busy himself addictively with ancient documents (and was known to be sceptical of professional fortune-tellers). The thing was, the old priest was intimidated by the idea of the great and unknown capital. He had no idea how to reach the scholars who worked for the king. They were important palace personnel, intent on their great work, and probably completely inaccessible to some country priest come from afar with a weight around his neck. But that stone would give him no peace.

It was still black when he went down to the river. He knew the fishers; one would steer him down to the main waterway where he could start his disjointed, awkward pilgrimage. As for Nineveh, he would worry about that when he got there.

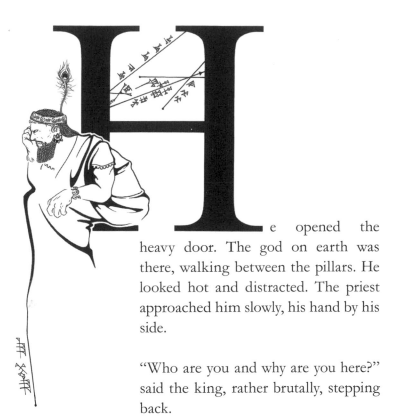

He opened the heavy door. The god on earth was there, walking between the pillars. He looked hot and distracted. The priest approached him slowly, his hand by his side.

"Who are you and why are you here?" said the king, rather brutally, stepping back.

He had thought himself alone, and was much preoccupied. His clothing was askew, too, and he was aware that at that moment he could hardly look like the king of all the world. He felt a deep sense of grievance at being disturbed. How did the fellow manage to be there?

"Where are my guards?"

"I have come in peace, my Lord and King," said the priest.

"*And*?" said the king.

"I have something for you, Greatness," said the priest, gravely. It seemed likely that the king would walk off at any minute, or call for a guardsman. They would spear him through at once.

"Not another *petition*, please," said the king. "Maybe an untried princess or two…?"

"It is written, my Lord. It is old."

"Oh, an old text that you have found. Good. Show it."

The priest held out his hand to the king, the stone on his open palm. He was trembling at his unforeseen proximity to the king's person.

The king plucked the misshapen egg from his hand without a word and turned it in his fingers, inspecting carefully, the intelligence lucid in his dark eyes.

"This is indeed a treasure. What is it, a nose from a statue? With writing *inside*? I must endeavour to read its message. Come tomorrow and I shall reward you appropriately. Find the major-domo when you come, tell him I want you."

* * *

The messenger came to the high gate of the College, and called to the janitor. The janitor locked the outer door on him, and went into the inner courtyard.

"What does he want now, his Exalted Highness?"

The First Exorcist was brought up short by the clear irritation in his own voice. He looked up. It was annoying to be interrupted, it always was, but for a moment he had let slip an impatience that should at any cost be hidden. It would be lost on the doorkeeper, of course, but he must be vigilant in all circumstances. He knew that the deep working of his inner self, free of discontent throughout his adult life, was delicately changing. His work nowadays was esoteric and complex and uninterrupted solitude in his chamber with his own library to hand was a rare commodity; but a summons from the king was paramount and he was always the first port of call. And the king's work was never uninteresting and often more than statecraft; the king had been obsessed with his library of all knowledge since his first ivory stylus inscribed with his name in ornate characters. The determined young prince had driven his first tutor into retirement, and never lost the taste for learning. It was a rare thing in a conquering king, secure on his throne, to be hunting tablets for his collection, the older the better, wanting to read everything for *himself*. In that, they were kindred. A very different creature from the usual warmongers, it had to be acknowledged, propelled by crudity and ignorance, or the whining hypochondriac who had been pulled every which way by his "advisors". It was impressive how the king squeezed it all in, what with the diplomats and the foreign missions, the generals and the lawyers, the nagging wheedlers and the hangers-on, and on top of it all, the astrologers and dream-merchants, the diviners, readers of entrails and students of the sky, who were all over the court; each with their own ancient traditions, their *most authentic* writings, and their own axe to grind. Through all these murky shallows the king steered a clear course, running household and empire with one hand, and reading over a lamp in the darkness, deliberating over old voices and forgotten authorities, even arguing on occasion with the professionals. That was a king for you.

And yet, there was something troublesome now bubbling under the surface of his private mind.

The janitor was holding the door.

"Some old bit of writing, my master. Someone with an eye on the main chance offered it to the king today. He loves it because he can't read a word, and wants to know what it says."

The First Exorcist climbed into the palanquin and tried to force his distracted mind into court procedure and protocol.

* * *

The king strode up to him.

"Look at this for me, will you? I have just acquired it for the Ancient Collection Room in the Library. You know how I value these old and curious writings. Now this is a piece for the true connoisseur. Look at these incredible tiny wedges. It is stone, is it not? But whose hand? And what signs are these? What does it mean, my learned scribe?"

"I must declare, my Lord, that I cannot quite decipher this inscription standing on my two feet. I must consider the matter at length. There are textual obscurities in profusion. My Lord is quite correct in pointing to the unusual nature of the –"

"Yes, yes, obviously. Well, look, take it with you by all means and read it, but bring it back tomorrow and explain it all to me, from head to foot."

The king moved impatiently as he spoke.

"Might my Lord confide in me whence this curiosity comes?"

"Some little priest up from the south brought it. He found it somewhere and brought it straight here to me. Arrived only this morning. He couldn't read it, of course, but he knew it must be important. He's coming back tomorrow to find out what it says and get his reward. I think he must be right. I've never seen anything like it."

The Exorcist was free to leave, then. It was clear that the king did not really want to part with his new acquisition overnight, but it was essential for him to be alone immediately with the thing. He dismissed the waiting bearers and made his way at his own pace through the streets and alleyways that led to the College, thinking hard. The stone was safe in the tablet wallet strapped across his under-tunic, and he poked at the hard irregular shape repeatedly as he walked so that it hurt his skin and proved that it had not somehow been lost.

* * *

The true significance of the king's new acquisition had been apparent to the First Exorcist the moment he saw it. The recognition that the myriad signs inside the stone were unknown and unreadable was instantaneous.

The implications were appalling. The very existence of the stone, an obviously divine object with a uniquely unreadable inscription, was a fatal threat to his authority and the entire traditional body of knowledge of which he was master. He perceived this at once with inescapable clarity, and he was staggered.

Only a god could write in stone like that.

The acknowledgement declared itself to him as he walked, as if spoken into his ear. Worse yet, the signs in this accursed thing seemed to be in layers like an onion, unknown signs on top of unknown signs, a system of unimaginable complexity with irretrievable depths of meaning. He felt the cherished balance inside his mind teeter.

Never had the Exorcist ever permitted himself a moment of self-delusion, and now he faced the predicament head on. His reputation, which reached far beyond the heartland even to colleges abroad, was fully justified. No scholar in the country knew the classics more perfectly, nor had greater knowledge of the signs themselves. Advanced students who read with him marvelled despairingly at his encyclopaedic knowledge. A difficult sign, an awkward word that defeated the assembled scholars would spark off in his mind a hundred literary associations, drawing on the oldest narratives, the rarest types of literature, the most esoteric of word lists. He knew it to be true that if he himself could not decipher the earth-shattering message stone, no other could possibly do so.

And what would happen to him? And them? Their expertise and exquisite scholarship, the fruit of uncounted centuries of intellectual enquiry, would be set at naught; the subtle, professional interpretations at which he was so gifted – and on which the kingdom often literally depended – would be devalued overnight. Derision would follow, and disgrace. The story would redound through ages to come.

Did you hear? The Royal Librarian received a personal message from the gods and his supposedly Expert Tablet Reader couldn't decipher a word of it!

There could be no conspiring to fool his lord and master, what was more, to manufacture some kind of credible interpretation. The king knew so much that there could be no deluding him.

The First Exorcist fell into a deep reverie, breathing slowly. He could feel himself closing in automatically, wrapping himself in a shield, a new hardness of purpose congealing like glass in his deepest mind. There was always a solution to be discovered by cold clarity, and his intelligence did not desert him. Three crucial factors had to be accommodated. He must find out where the stone came from. He must make the priest disappear completely, leaving no trace whatsoever. And the stone must be completely destroyed, in a way that would be accepted unhesitatingly by the king, with no lasting effects.

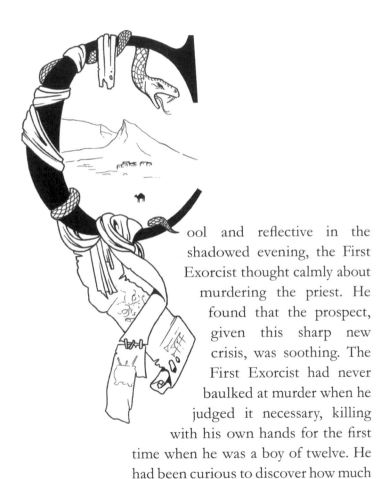

ool and reflective in the shadowed evening, the First Exorcist thought calmly about murdering the priest. He found that the prospect, given this sharp new crisis, was soothing. The First Exorcist had never baulked at murder when he judged it necessary, killing with his own hands for the first time when he was a boy of twelve. He had been curious to discover how much pressure was needed to choke the life out of a person, so he strangled a small girl, discovering thereby that there was also an uncharted and unexpected excitement when life shuddered into bird-like brokenness. No one ever connected him with her death, which left him at the very outset of his quite abnormal career free of inhibition and of the fear of discovery.

The girl in this first case happened to be his sister. He had simply left her body behind some old houses, two of which were uninhabited. Her discovery had provoked the inevitable intense wailing and mourning from the family women. The men were more inclined to shrug it off; no one thought for a moment that the death was anything but an accident. The child had fallen awkwardly when running or playing in poor light. No one had seen anything; no one came forward. Little girls were hardly in short supply, anyway. But there was no trouble either when he later killed two more children.

* * *

The successful young murderer immersed himself in the scribal school curriculum with an adult level of concentration and understanding that astonished his teachers, perfecting his control of the stylus on clay, so that he could produce immaculate calligraphy or imitate a variety of ancient hands at will.

The school was in a small town in the north. The head of the institution had already remarked that the boy should soon be thinking of going to the capital, or, better still, south to Babylon. He himself had been in slight fear of his brilliant student for some time and for a whole group of reasons one afternoon suddenly made up his mind to arrange the transfer as soon as possible.

The boy knew nothing of the great city or what he would encounter there. The other pupils, of whom there were eight, had been intimates since the beginning, destined to become high-ranking scribes. They were defensive in the face of the new arrival, especially since his mastery of the literature was already profound and all too evident. The ability to interpret old or obscure texts bestowed an inestimable advantage on any candidate for promotion, for professional work often involved finding convincing meaning on the spot when the future needed to be predicted, in the impatient company of generals or the king himself. Most diviners had their own specialisation, like movement of the stars, or how to interpret the flight of a specially liberated bird, but the newcomer, with his voracious appetite for knowledge, seemed to have everything already tidily stored in his head. What made him so remarkable was that his mastery extended to the deepest works on magic and medicine. Before long, he could never be bested in interpretation or understanding, and just when they had all decided that he had made everything clear, they would learn that the real meaning was directly the opposite.

Only one pupil had ever emerged to challenge him in the cool rooms of the college. This boy, an orphan of much the same age, had an uncanny flair for reading broken signs or deciphering old and worn fragments, and he was called on automatically even by the scholars to help with difficult passages. This engendered violent resentment in the young Exorcist, for he knew that his own abilities in this direction too were, if anything, superior. He was quite unaware that his teachers understood this perfectly and were deliberate in their behaviour, but as time passed the matter became intolerable to him. The best solution long eluded him, but then it came to him that what he needed was some means to blind his rival.

It was nearly a month before the method, simple in the extreme, came to him. Their training included accurate observations of phenomena in the heavens: first and last visibilities, the zodiac combinations, the behaviour of the major planets; the details to be learned were endless. For centuries, the training of apprentice observers in the Academy had benefited from carved wooden tubes, hollow throughout and of a diameter to fit the eye comfortably. These devices enabled the watcher to focus more clearly on a specific point and see more clearly by eliminating the surrounding backdrop. The sky tubes were stored on a shelf in a small room at the top of the observation tower where they studied the changing intricacies of the heavens through the night and drew the patterns. These tubes were very old, fashioned of shiny wood with a tarnished copper ring at each end. Such a tube, he thought, furnished a handy means of application. In a week's time each young scholar was scheduled to spend one night in turn up there and, using a lamp, draw out on a clay tablet whatever sky section his tutor demanded. If something could be introduced into the star tube lying waiting on the table, that substance would slide straight into the eye as soon as the instrument was raised into position. A small scorpion, a deadly worm, a certain burning poison…

A wrenching scream woke the other candidates towards the second watch of that night. The Head of Medicine washed the eye with quickening Tigris water seven and seven times and applied several soothing agents but the sight was lost; they crowded round the table in horror to inspect the whitened, sightless eye of their colleague. The misfortune was unexplained; the gods must have had some reason. Two days later he was gone from the college; a scribe had to be perfect in body as well as mind. In after years, they learned, he became an engraver of stone seals and produced many children.

* * *

In time, killing without hesitation had become part of his work. As a known specialist, he had once been summoned across town at night by a midwife then unknown to him. She had been struggling for hours to deliver a dreadful, abnormal foetus that had come to term, and sent for him in desperation. Huge and bloated, it had been stuck fast since the morning in a half-born state. The midwife had determined that the anomaly had grotesque, overdeveloped shoulders with extra bone outgrowth that could never pass down the birth canal. The feet that protruded were scaly and hairy, with webbed toes, the worst case of misbegotten horror that he had either witnessed or read about. The mother, a girl of about eighteen, was beyond any help they could offer. But, as she screamed and twisted in visceral agony, she jerked herself briefly into an upright position and caught a glimpse of the grotesque, inhuman feet sticking out below between her thighs. Before their very eyes her brain cracked into bottomless insanity. Without hesitation, the young Exorcist had bent over the bed and broken her slippery neck with an economy of movement that would itself have terrified the midwife had she not already been on the point of fainting. In unspoken agreement, they cut the atrocious, twitching thing out of its dead mother's body, limb by limb, until it was possible to pull out the remainder in one lump. The midwife stared at the dismembered foetus in disbelief: it seemed to be a cross between a monkey and a bat.

The Exorcist took her firmly by the shoulders and forced her to look up at him. He had smears of blood on his forehead.

"Clean her up for her husband to be able to see her. Wash her, stitch her, tidy her in white cloth. Tell him she died because of the gods with her purity intact and that no mother could have done more to bring a child into the world. And tell him it was a girl. He won't mind so much. He can remarry. I shall deal with this thing and do what is necessary. Later, one will come to purify the chamber. Wait for him. And never speak of what has happened here."

Moving swiftly by alleyways and small streets he had taken the pieces in a plaited reed bag to a smithy. There, they worked for the army and their furnaces never cooled; undernourished campaign slaves worked through the nights forging swords, spears and pieces of armour. No one made any comment when he crossed the workshop floor and cast the bag and its contents unceremoniously into the white heat, muttering certain formulae below his breath. Purification by the same fire that produced the keenest edges for the state's weapons was recommended for such things. Nothing would remain, and no trouble would come to the premises. But, before leaving, he had touched the Chief Smith fleetingly on the forehead and made some discreet movement with his hands. The man, steaming and half-naked in the din, said nothing, but he could see in his eyes that his gesture had left reassurance. He knew then for the first time that power floated in the world to be harnessed, and that he could achieve it.

* * *

Arriving now at a death sentence for the priest thus gave him no pause. He could not avoid taking the Second Exorcist into his confidence up to a point, but no one else would see the full picture, or so much as glimpse the deep, black plans that he could feel all the time seething and swirling up in his mind.

Now that the stone had arrived, nothing would ever be the same again, for anyone.

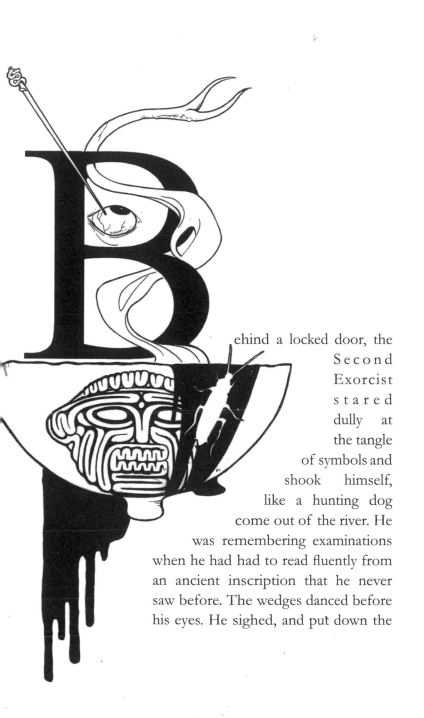

Behind a locked door, the Second Exorcist stared dully at the tangle of symbols and shook himself, like a hunting dog come out of the river. He was remembering examinations when he had had to read fluently from an ancient inscription that he never saw before. The wedges danced before his eyes. He sighed, and put down the stone. It reposed aggressively, jagged and asymmetrical on a fragment of red ritual cloth. The redness gleamed under the great oil lamps like a pool of blood to be shed. The First Exorcist went over the main points of their predicament without drawing the final conclusion, but his deputy was quick to meet him.

"So, we kill him, then?"

"We kill him, for certain. Thrice over, do we kill him."

"How thrice?" asked the Third Exorcist thoughtlessly. He was a brilliant scholar, with a brilliant career no doubt ahead of him, but he had been seen to lack in part the crucial worldliness that his elders possessed in abundance. They ignored him. Undeclared, the two older Exorcists were moving into a new alliance. Their eyes met across the light, the faint promise of shared violence between them. Their colleague might possibly, could just possibly, condemn himself. Now he must be given another task. The First slid over a small, unbaked tablet.

"Here is a recipe. Make it up exactly downstairs, into sweetened cakes. Bring them to me when they are ready."

The Second Exorcist pulled the heavy, embroidered wall hanging dismissively across the doorway, and spoke low to his colleague.

"Continue. The night presses in."

"The heart of it is," pursued the First Exorcist, "that no one else in the city but the king knows anything about the stone. The bumpkin had the wit to sense something of what he had found, and hurried here immediately like a delirious squirrel with a Syrian walnut to show *His Majesty*. Probably expected to get a sack of gold for his pains. Now he will just get the pains."

"But we need to discover where he got the accursed stone before he dies. *And are there any more?*"

"I have looked, with the smoke. Deep have I looked. There was a dead man. From that dead man to our little priest. The dead man was a strong Magician. He is still strong. The stone I saw with him for many years. From a plain across mountains, towards the home of the sun. I could see no further back. But there are no other stones."

"Then the secret can die with the rustic."

"Just so."

"The burning?"

"Burning, poison and knives. He must be extinguished completely, like kindling in a brazier. His body must vanish, all trace of him, his clothes, his seal, everything that was his, as if he was never born of his mother. We'll start the process now. It is the third watch."

He paused, and lowered his voice.

"There is one old tablet I have to fetch. It is from Babylon. There is… a collection of certain manuscripts and pieces of apparatus in a baked clay chest that passes from First Exorcist to First Exorcist, which, under normal circumstance, can be shown to no other person. They are not kept in our library, but hidden in my own chambers. I have read them all, of course. They are for… *killing* magic. From earlier times, Hammurabi probably, or even older. One is exceptionally remarkable, and contains certain spells that no one today can understand. It is magic likewise from beyond the mountains, from the East. It is like our *Burning*, but slower and more time-consuming."

"Time is what we do not have, however."

"We have sufficient. You will come with me."

"And the *body*?"

The First Exorcist leaned forward.

"I have an idea. It is clean. But we will need silver. Get it as usual."

The curtain swayed behind them and they fell silent immediately. The Third Exorcist entered quietly with a black stone bowl containing the desired sweetmeats. The First Exorcist examined them carefully and nodded dismissively.

He covered the bowl and rang the ornate tall bell on the table for his servant. The man came in. He was stunted in size, almost yellow-skinned, with a repellent hare lip. He was practically inarticulate, but with sharp hearing and a great and fostered intelligence. But for his obvious physical impurities, the Exorcist would long ago have taught him to read and practice his own craft. He had served his master since his earliest years with extreme devotion, and was consequently privy to many secrets and had seen many things.

The Exorcist instructed this ally with the minimum of speech. He was to recruit a particular young priestess well known to them both from the neighbouring College. She should be well wrapped up against prying eyes and completely unidentifiable afterwards. She was to go to all the places where a poor out-of-town priest might find lodging for a few nights. (He must have walked there from the palace. There were not so many possibilities.) Look till he is found; sell or give him a cake. Send her alone, but follow her yourself secretly till she is returned. Bring me a description of the buffalo as soon as you can. A *name* if possible, or a *bit* of something…"

The servant nodded and slipped out silently.

Across town, the country priest was seated tranquilly against the pilaster at the back wall in his room. He was marvelling to himself that he had seen the Great King in his Palace and conversed with him, and that the king had taken his stone into his own safekeeping. This was surely the work of the gods, who had supervised his journey from afar at every stage, guarding him from drowning or being robbed, or losing his way. The story of his journey would be a lasting fireside narrative on his return. He must take care to remember every detail. He had not remarked the king's surprising untidiness nor his human signs of discomfiture. A great weight had passed from his mind, while the promise that there would be gold for him on the morrow left him completely unmoved. He would take it home safely for the temple, of course. There were many ways in which the two of them could take such munificence and do good with it.

The silent, bent woman with a tray of small dark cakes went slowly from room to room in the caravanserai, and paused in the doorway, looking expectantly for the old priest. Her surprisingly youthful eyes glittered uncomfortably at him but he did not notice anything unusual. He just smiled at her and took one through kindness. He would eat it later. After his prayers of thankfulness.

The swathed, unspeaking woman walked quickly away from the old building. Her shadowy follower had paused to scrutinise the priest himself, but no one there knew his name and the room was empty of possessions. The priest had little hair and he could think of no way of obtaining one from the living head, while the dust in the room must be from a thousand other inhabitants. He would return…

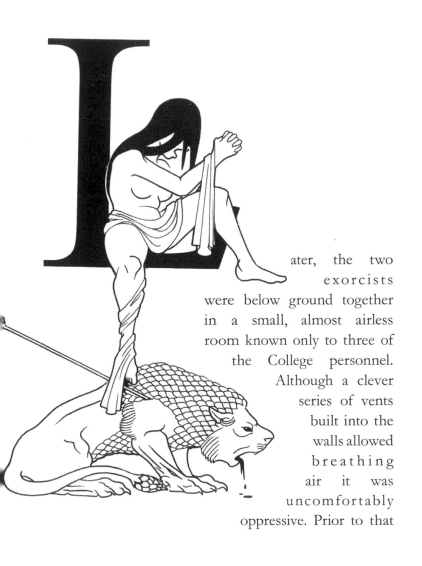

ater, the two exorcists were below ground together in a small, almost airless room known only to three of the College personnel. Although a clever series of vents built into the walls allowed breathing air it was uncomfortably oppressive. Prior to that evening, no one had set foot in it for more than a decade. An unidentifiable smell was pervasive, and soon more than unpleasant. There was a packet of worked potter's clay waiting on the bench. The First Exorcist had long ago taken the precaution of bribing a royal eunuch to procure one of the queen's gold hairpins in the conviction that, sooner or later, it would be useful. He was now sharpening it on the ancient whetstone which lay to hand on the basement table, together with an assortment of other materials that would scarcely be recognised by people hurrying in the everyday world above their heads.

The Second Exorcist was soon at work on the figurine. He was skilful; it would be no grotesque mannequin, but a well-proportioned likeness of the country priest as described to him; of middle age, plump and unshapely but not gross, with little hair and a weak left leg. The figure grew under his fingers, with its simple garb that he reproduced in a twist of cloth and a belt. They stood him up on the bench, and added a splash of paint. A very small stone was pressed into his left hand. The figure looked back at them, placid and trusting.

The ancient tablet that emerged from the coffer was wrapped many times in bands of stained cloth. The First Exorcist shielded the tablet with his body from his colleague's eyes, but the latter could see that it was of a rare, black clay, in minute writing, with tiny drawings each with its caption. The First Exorcist had brought down a fragile-looking and obviously foreign shawl. He now drew the moth-eaten fabric over his head, covering his head and shoulders completely. Crouched on the floor, he began to intone the first incantation almost inaudibly, reading fluently from the angular script, addressing not the gods of light who created and protected, but an alien dark god with a tortuous, barbaric name.

The atmosphere grew more oppressive as the coals in a small brass tripod began to glow. A heady, costly incense began to fill the room. The two men stood together in the gloom, their hands configured in some strange and unnatural pose, their eyes fixed on the figure through the swirling, perfumed smoke. The First Exorcist began to intone the next recitation, squinting through the billows to make out the signs. He pronounced each phrase in a whisper; each repeated by his colleague. They worked through the sequence of spells seven times each. Then the Second Exorcist seized hold of the figure. The First Exorcist raised the sharpened needle of gold and drove it violently through the chest of the miniature priest. Then he drove a silver pin into the groin. Finally, using a toothed device with hinged bronze jaws he crushed the head. They stood it back up and waited.

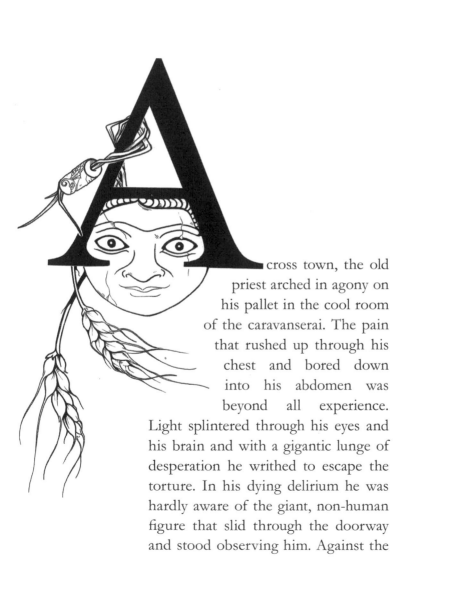

cross town, the old priest arched in agony on his pallet in the cool room of the caravanserai. The pain that rushed up through his chest and bored down into his abdomen was beyond all experience. Light splintered through his eyes and his brain and with a gigantic lunge of desperation he writhed to escape the torture. In his dying delirium he was hardly aware of the giant, non-human figure that slid through the doorway and stood observing him. Against the light, his vast shoulders seemed to be ringed with celestial rays of brightness. The old priest knew then that the figure must be a divine messenger, and that the immense power of the hands that were lifting him from the bedding like a sheaf of straw to snap his spine was ordained by ineluctable fate, and that his time had indeed come. A fleeting last insight struck him as the final pain began, that he would be unable to make his appointment on the next day with the King of the World.

It was the great Butcher-Cook from the College, deaf and dumb from birth, one-eyed but with the strength of several men, who stood there. His equally speechless partner who had brought him was himself a mannequin beside him. The Cook rolled up the body in its covering and hoisted it effortlessly onto his shoulder, while the other collected the bag and sandals and made a rapid check; the priest had no other possessions to account for.

The Cook walked out of the room as if he were a carpenter carrying a roof beam. No one observed the giant with his burden – or if they did, they made no remark and forgot what they had seen. He was dressed in a long black garment that flowed around him as he walked, noiselessly and with surprising lightness. He, like the companion at his knee, belonged to the First Exorcist personally. He, too, had been purchased as a child, already outsized, after years of cruelty and persecution. He had six toes on his left foot, and one or two other unconventional features known only to his master. The mother, a diseased slave of unknown origin, had handed him over gratefully for a handful of silver scraps and vanished for good. As was his way, the Exorcist had chosen wisely. The giant worked in the kitchens, cutting up the meat that he brought from the market as whole sides for the student stews. His were the heavy jobs around the College but, most importantly, he followed the First Exorcist as attendant or bodyguard whenever needed and did whatever he was instructed. Sometimes, deep in the night, the Exorcist had coaxed sounds out of him, patiently leading him to refine the few rudimentary noises of which he was capable. The Cook knew he was safe for life, and that his master was looking for the correct magic to let him speak words. He had been told the task was immense and might still take years, and that he must be patient.

The great knife and solid blows made short work of the fleshy priest and the long bones were soon broken up. The Cook crushed the skull and other easily recognisable parts, and stowed the dismembered portions in one of the huge, greased sacks used for his market runs. He washed down the table and salt-scrubbed it in three directions. One of the priests would always come down later for a conventional purification if asked.

Long after nightfall, the Cook made his way on foot through the dark passages carrying the priest on a journey he had made before. He paused once, standing completely still in the quiet, judging his moment before tossing the dismemberment knife out into the river.

The keepers of the king's lions lived in a permanent encampment. There were three of them, one known especially well to the Cook. There was nodded agreement, and the sack passed from one shoulder to another. A glint of heavy silver gleamed briefly in the moonlight. They grinned at one another in the dark, and there was a long flask of wine to hand.

The priest's clothes and other pieces were all burnt to nothing in the College basement. That left only his cylinder seal. It was poorly cut, but a good stone. It was taken by the servile dwarf to the covered market where the seal-cutters worked, ground down to smoothness in a back room and tossed into a box of blanks, to be inscribed afresh one day for some rich merchant in town on a spending spree.

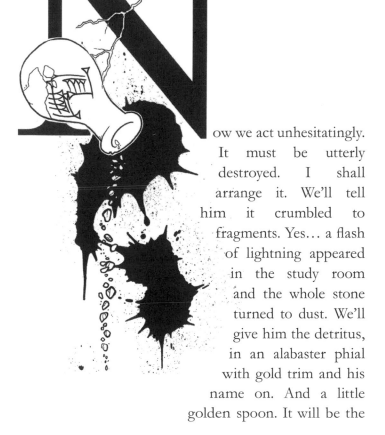

ow we act unhesitatingly. It must be utterly destroyed. I shall arrange it. We'll tell him it crumbled to fragments. Yes… a flash of lightning appeared in the study room and the whole stone turned to dust. We'll give him the detritus, in an alabaster phial with gold trim and his name on. And a little golden spoon. It will be the rarest medicine in the world. We'll call it *mountain dust*. Specially recommended for aging monarchs anxious for a strong new heir. Beyond the resources of a king's treasury…"

The First Exorcist laughed in exhilaration; his colleague nodded, shocked at the uncharacteristic outburst but convinced, likewise, that the stone must disappear. The other would do it very efficiently, he knew, and they would never refer to it again.

Now it was time to drink.

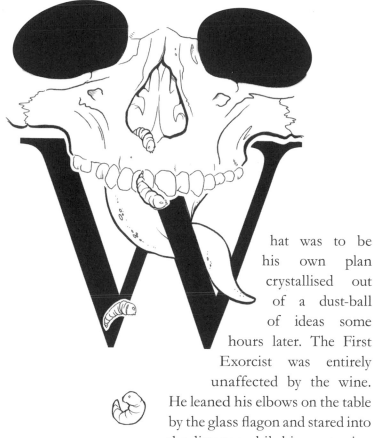

hat was to be his own plan crystallised out of a dust-ball of ideas some hours later. The First Exorcist was entirely unaffected by the wine. He leaned his elbows on the table by the glass flagon and stared into the distance while his companion dozed unheedingly.

The first insight was that the writing stone could not be destroyed, but must be hidden with complete safety until he was ready to make use of it. Already, half-articulated, he could envision how it might be used and what he might accomplish with it, but the timing would need to be judged by a hair. The second point was that he would have to absent himself on a trip. Possibly quite protracted. In fact, as he followed the now rapid workings of his own mind, he must take the stone with him. It must never be out of his control, and anyway he would need it with him. Certain was that. And he would have first to manipulate the king – not for the first time – and also set things up so that the College would run smoothly until his return. Finally, he must make sure that any leftover dangers were removed. That young nun would have to go. He looked down disdainfully at the Second Exorcist, sprawled in ungainly oblivion across the table. He had no choice now but to leave the man in charge. His hands would be full with demands from the palace, anyway. But perhaps the clever thing would be to lead the Second Exorcist to the conviction that, during his absence, he must dispose of their unreliable under-colleague for *his* own safety. He nodded, as if persuaded by an outside voice. He would hypnotise him before leaving.

But there would still be danger, for his future Deputy alone knew of the stone and memory of it could not be reliably dislodged by working or suggestion. Ultimately he would have to settle that too. It could be the final leak through which damned-up waters could one day pour through in a rage of destruction and confound his plans. The Exorcist would take the Cook south with him but leave the Dwarf behind, with instructions to orchestrate the first killing and otherwise use his judgment as to the second, charged with his own secret authority. The Dwarf would do everything necessary.

Somewhere in the drugs room there was an unusual little vessel in a poor-quality crystal, and he remembered a piece of some foreign yellow stone that would do perfectly. He found it still in the marble chest, wrapped in goatskin, but it resisted the hand-mortar and would have to be crushed with the great millstone downstairs. A few grains of stimulant could go in, for a convincing bit of aftertaste. It wouldn't kill His Majesty anyway, one measure every other day before the sun rises, kneeling to the east and whispering something suitable. A little beer would wash it down and a quick rub with oil could follow. He would jot something down on a little recipe tablet for his master. And suggest the alluring spectacle of a whole row of swelling nubile bellies in the months to come.

* * *

"It vanished completely?" said the king incredulously. "In a flash of light? What can this mean? Had you read the signs for me?"

"Only the… outer ring. It was full of meaning. *Truth, kingship, ages for all time…*"

"And it *vanished*? This is intolerable. Think what might hinge on it. A dynastic message from the Highest Authority. From the gods' council direct, for once; where else? Can nothing be done to… bring it back?"

"I have all the essence in this old crystal bottle. The golden residue. It will be possessed of special power, of course. According to an old tablet I read many years ago, a lightning-struck stone is full of regenerative power. You remember that pebble that was found once with a frog inside? Very costly, even for a few grains. A parallel and venerable tradition."

"Yes. I remember. It made no difference, though."

"But you are of the heroic build of kings, my Lord. We had but a pinch of the stuff. I have a proposal, my Lord. The priest who saw you, I will go back with him to his village, and investigate the source of this stone. It seemed to me when reading it that perhaps there are others and that they must be read together, somehow interlocked to give the message. Perhaps that priest brought us just one as a sample. I can seek out all the others, bring them here and we can decipher them in privacy. *Together.* And get the all the meanings for you. After all, no mysterious-looking text has ever defeated us, has it, my Lord?"

"This is a good plan. If there are more, you will get them. Take whatever gold you need. We must have those writings at any expense. And write down for me what you can remember of the first one, that the gods took back. Perhaps it means that there is a better message to come. Yes, that must be it. Anyway, go with discretion and bring me swiftly the remainder. You will be away some time, therefore?"

"All arrangements will be in place, my Lord. My colleague will attend to all as usual. I will need time free if I am to travel far."

"Do what is needful, and when you are successful you can send me news under safe words, "the harvest is good", or some such. I shall be much exercised about these stones until we have them here and have wrested their meaning from within them."

"As you command so will I do; if your stones exist, so will I bring them."

The First Exorcist knew to leave his king then, still holding the fake bottle of mountain dust, outlined against the tapestry hangings, august and upright. He walked quietly backwards towards the familiar inner door. It crossed his mind to wonder as he reached the doorway whether he would ever see the king of the universe again.

Probably not, he thought.

They would depart the capital long before dawn. He would travel as the same type of healer as found the stone. With a thinned beard, a painted scar at the temple and rough clothing he would be unrecognisable; a loose cloak could easily be swept in front of his face or over his head. The Cook would always be behind him, at a distance, on the alert. They would go south by river.

t was the correct temple, he knew. They crossed the courtyard in the darkness and the Exorcist opened the door into the inner chamber. There was no one present, but a row of oil lamps threw shifting shadows onto the shining image of the goddess looking down on them. Behind him, he heard the Cook sighing, and he turned to see his companion with his hands outstretched towards the figure. The Exorcist grimaced. He must find this second priest quickly. It was better to deal with such matters at night, after travelling inconspicuously by day. On impulse, he went up to the statue to examine the array of small figurines, votive amulets, models of breast or leg deposited there by the locals. The low shelf was cluttered, and many items must have lain there for years. He was looking for something, without certainty of what it would be, but he knew immediately when he saw the little ivory goddess tucked in at the edge that she must have belonged to the Healer. He concealed it deftly under his cloak. There was nothing else there that could have conceivably come from the same source, but he knew they would have collected all the tools of his profession and perhaps they had not buried them with the corpse. He stepped into the adjoining chambers and looked around. There were only the trappings that these small-time priests would use in their rituals. He would have to interrogate the incumbent quickly.

They found the hut. The young priest lay asleep, alone. The Exorcist stood tilting the priest's own lamp over the bed until he came awake. He sat up abruptly in his sheepskin and asked with a stammer what they wanted. The Exorcist waited a long time without speaking. He could see the blossoming fear in the eyes of the priest, who made as if to rise from his bedding. The Exorcist at once forced him down with his iron left hand and kept him pinned by the sternum while the other looked back at him in stark terror, his yellow eyes like a toad's under a rock. With his right hand, the Exorcist slowly drew a thin, silvery dagger from the folds of his cloak. The priest cried out then, in sheer panic, at which the spectral figure of the Cook, hitherto invisible, stepped out of the darkness and stood behind his master. He, too, was completely silent. The priest started to babble some ineffective prayer to the inert stone deity across the way to whom he had prayed a thousand times for protection against evil without having the slightest understanding of what the word could mean. The Exorcist raised the dagger slowly. The priest wet himself.

"I have come for my brother's possessions. The Healer. You have them. Fetch them."

He adjusted the blade so that the

lamplight caught it and the weapon gleamed in polished malevolence. The mind of the priest was almost shut down in its fear, but the memory of his vanished colleague stowing the bag with his back turned came back to him. The cursed things were in a trunk behind the cella in the little store. The reeking apprentice pointed and the Exorcist stepped back in distaste. The priest staggered out into the temple and they followed him through the narrow disguised door into the rear chamber. The chest was soon unroped. The bag was hidden at the bottom under a heap of coloured banners embroidered with the image of the goddess used for a festival. The priest was shaking so badly that he dropped the bag. The Exorcist hissed with impatience and knelt on the beaten floor to examine it. It was tied at the neck, and he could feel the contents unyielding through the material. He stood up slowly and looked once at the Cook. The Cook picked up the skinny priest and threw him bodily into the chest. Then they stuffed down the pile of textiles around and on top of him and shut the lid. As they retied the ropes there was no sound from within. They pushed the chest against the far wall and the Cook dumped several baskets and an old stone grinder for good measure on top.

"He'll dry out like an Egyptian," said the Exorcist.

They closed the door behind them and went out into the warm darkness.

* * *

There was no one to observe the two men silhouetted against the sweep of the dark sky as they approached the cemetery, carrying their stolen irrigation spades in silence. The man at the front paused by the gate. The whole area was surrounded by a reed and mud wall, delineated against accidental trespass or, rather, perhaps to keep the inhabitants within. There were bumps across the ground, but few clear signs of where one grave might have encroached on another, and little indication that the deceased were visited regularly by those whom they had left behind. Not everyone buried their dead here; some preferred the closeness of interring their deceased family members under their house floors. Miscellaneous other types came to rest here, no-good women, thieves, people left on their own, and dead strangers.

The Cook followed after his master and almost bumped into him, for he had stopped abruptly for no obvious reason. It was his master alone who had observed the stone-still sentinel he had been half-anticipating, a green, sharp-toothed, flying creature that crouched immobile over the flattened earth, its protective wings fully-extended, trembling very slightly at the tip. Here, then, the Healer must be buried.

The Exorcist was not remotely intimidated by the presence of the Healer's guardian. He felt under his clothing and produced the jagged fragment of crystal that he had found in the bag. He stood straight up, pointed the crystal at the creature and uttered two clear lines from an ancient banishing ritual as an opening gambit. The scaly being raised its head and looked at him. Then, as if grown suddenly old, it closed its eyes, slowly lifted its wings and rose into the sky. It hovered above the two men, sparkling from the moon, and began to circle above their heads in a leisurely way, flitting from the darkness into moments of light and then was gone again. The Exorcist pointed to where the digging should begin.

The Cook removed most of his clothing and lifted the little spade. He dug neatly, depositing the spoil carefully for quick replacement. Before long, he came down on the burial jar.

The body was only partially decomposed. The Cook knelt and seized hold so that he could jerk the body out of the jar in one movement. It flew up in a stench and landed like a fish at the feet of the triumphant Exorcist. The violence of the interment had forced the long bones to burst through the joints. The eyes were long gone and maggots in profusion were hard at work in the brain cavity. The Cook detached the head as if following detailed instructions. As he did so, the silence of the world was shattered by a high, unwavering scream from the Healer's green watchman.

Overhead came the flapping of parchment wings beating against the air, and the Exorcist looked up to see a blanket of great eagles, interlocked in flight, their hunter's instinct finely tuned. They in turn took up a violent screeching, and flew lower and lower towards him until they were just out of reach. The Exorcist stood up and stretched out his arms, his fingers splayed in a command of dismissal. Then his own voice was to be heard against the blur of their wings and the racket of their cries, a recitation into the night sky of a spell no one had ever heard pronounced aloud in the capital. At that, all the birds fell to the ground as if stoned by a battalion of slingsmen, their shuddering bodies like damp leaves covering and recovering the headless corpse.

The Exorcist began to peel the remaining skin off the Healer's skull, spreading out the strips and fragments to dry. The maggots and beetles poured out of the eyeholes seeking refuge or oblivion in the dust. The Exorcist pulled away such tendons and muscles as had resisted the insects until the skull was more or less naked and white, and ready for use. Watched carefully by the Cook he then cut the genitalia from the body and wrapped them up in some pieces of the shroud. The Cook stuffed the remains back into the jar and re-covered the whole until the ground, stamped well down, looked as it had before. The Cook carried the skull and other trophies as they made their way down to the nearest canal. There was a need for water.

Behind them, unnoticed, the green creature landed mournfully on the freshly trodden earth and resumed its immobile position.

* * *

The barn was full of stores but little that was edible. The Exorcist gestured to the Cook that he should go and find food and drink somewhere, taking his time; he would undoubtedly be needing a woman. The great dark figure slipped out into the darkness and the Exorcist was alone for the first time in many days.

Working swiftly, he cleared a space against the eastern wall of the building and made a structure out of three sacks, two for the base, one laid widthways across them. In the middle of the upper sack he placed the healer's skull, on top of a pile of grain. He sat before his trophy, cross-legged in concentration. He had made up in advance the recipe for the secret oil with which the skull had to be anointed, and there was olive oil in abundance to feed the wick of the miniature obsidian observation lamp that was also needed. He placed the lamp before the skull and filled it to the brim. Then, beginning the preliminary incantation under his breath, he unstoppered the phial and poured the oil delicately along the cranial fissure, south to north. The heavy oil stayed in position, and he worked it over the whole and down the sides to the jaws. A solitary maggot fell from between the teeth and he crushed it with a fingertip. The skull gleamed dully in the little pool of light. Next, the Exorcist sprinkled mixed sulphur and myrrh over the flame, and re-seated himself before the skull. There were several long invocations that he had learned off by heart before departing from the College. The Sun God was being steadily coerced into summoning the shade of the dead man to enter the skull and answer questions reliably. The Exorcist cradled his temples in his oily fingertips and stared into the black eye-sockets before him, concentrating and compelling with the full force of his being. At length, he felt the incipient presence of the spirit that was unable to resist the remorseless tugging, and prepared himself to frame his first question. His voice was low but as penetrating and as cold as death.

"Are you come?"

He waited. There was no sound but the remote lowing of cattle somewhere behind the barn. Eventually, he saw the skull's lower jaw twitch and the teeth part, and then the voice came, echoing and reluctant.

"I… am… come."

"You are shackled by me."

"I… am… shackled."

"You must answer with truth."

"I will answer."

"Where did you procure the stone?"

The teeth of the upper and lower jaw ground together. The Exorcist waited.

"Over the plains and the mountain. By foot and on donkeys. A month. Two months' journey. A small town."

"What is it called?"

There was a pause.

"I do not remember. It was to the east and north of… Susa."

"Tell everything."

"There was a market. I was looking for gems. A fellow from the north had it. A musician. A lyre player. He found the stone in the north."

"Why did he show it to you?"

"Someone there said I could read. He wanted to know what was written."

Despite himself the Exorcist felt a twinge of fellowship with the disembodied wanderer.

"How many musicians?"

"Three. Lyre. Flute. Drum. They go everywhere."

"What further do you know?"

There was silence. The Exorcist crumbled something more into the lamp flame and bent forward.

"Well? Must I ask twice?"

"He said he had heard there was also a... cave."

"A cave?"

"With this writing in it. Everywhere. On the walls."

The Exorcist bent forward and waited. This was not at all what he had anticipated.

"Where is it?"

"Beyond the northern provinces."

"I need more. Where is that cave?"

"He did not tell me. Far to the north. In a fold of the mountains."

"Think of what he said or I will not release you."

There was a long sigh, almost inaudible.

"He said… the mountain was bent like a felt cap."

"What was it called?"

"I know no more. He was never in the cave. There was a man with a bag of things. He bought it. Years ago, maybe."

"What is the name of the musician?"

"I do not know."

"Describe him."

"He has very long hair."

"What is your name?"

"I... have... forgotten," came the whispered answer.

The Exorcist gestured in irritation. Did that, in fact, matter? He could describe the Healer well enough when it came to it...

Behind him, the Cook blundered in with his arms full of loot. He kicked the reed door shut behind him and came over to his master. He was full of mysterious energy.

The Exorcist stood up swiftly and took down the skull and covered it with some sacking. He could try again later if necessary.

"There is dried meat and bread and much more. Eat your fill, Master. And here, beer. It is good."

There were no words but the sense of the blunt gestures was lucid. They sat together on the floor. There was suddenly the fierce barking of at least two dogs, and a burly man appeared at the door and shouted at them. The

Exorcist took no notice but the Cook stood up and reached for his staff. The two great dogs charged across the floor and with wide swinging movements he killed the first and knocked the second unconscious. The farmer rushed over in a blind fury and charged at the Cook, who stumbled for a moment, knocking the oil lamp off the sacking. The oil ran across the floor. With a vengeful roar of his own, the Cook split the farmer's skull open, but within moments the room was ablaze, the piled sacks of dried materials kindling instantly. The Exorcist calmly swept up his possessions and the two men retreated outside, where they were met by the screaming wife of the farmer, and what was presumably the daughter. The Exorcist ignored the women and turned his back, busying himself in packing the skull and the other equipment carefully into his bag; he had lost his treasured old lamp for certain. He heard behind him the Cook cracking the two women's heads together and throwing them to the ground. Within minutes, as the Exorcist knew he would, he had raped them both, the mother once and the younger woman twice. There was no noise from either; perhaps they were already dead. Behind them, the fire spread to the other nearby buildings.

Animals were screaming now in the smoke. The Cook stood up and lifted both the ravaged women like bundles of cloth. He carried them towards the new part of the fire and threw them in. He dusted his hands together, and picked up his stick and shoulder bag. The two men walked unhurriedly together away from the scene.

"We could have had cooked meat instead of that dried stuff," said the Exorcist aloud, but the Cook, as usual, heard nothing.

e heard talk of a low-level merchant caravan, straggly and without paid sword bearers, travelling due east to Susa. To join it was uncomplicated; the leaders eyed the Exorcist, partly cloak-covered, without placing him, but welcomed the Cook for his evident prowess with a staff; no one would be troubling them as they journeyed.

The merchants were mostly on donkeys. The Cook tried one briefly, but his legs hung down too far and anyway he could walk faster than the dejected beast that he had been offered. He was now striding out somewhere at the rear of the column, clasping his wood. The Exorcist, precisely aware of how far away he was, was with a group of seasoned mountain people, not speaking, but concentrating unnoticed on their dialect. They were no speakers of Semitic, but some northern speech that he had encountered years before in an affable court ambassador, who had taught him fifty or so words which he wrote down with translations. He could follow now in part; he knew, for instance, that they were talking about him and wondering why he was travelling, but much of it was muttered and probably colloquial. He wanted to identify anything that they found remarkable about him so that he could downplay or alter it; the plan was to pass everywhere unnoticed, and he must learn to walk with less of a straight back, staring down, hiding his eyes. For now, he knew even without a mirror, the promise of violence shone out from those eyes in warning; the membrane of courtly respect and gravity that had always masked what lay within him

like the languid eyelids of a lizard was
gone. He must be a lone, forgettable
wanderer of few words, hearkening
to some inner voice, with that huge,
dogged shadow behind him, protective
and unspeaking.

It pleased him, as they made their way
unsteadily forward, to think of his
College in the sun-filled streets of the
capital, his staff about their prescribed
tasks, the emergency councils with the
king's diviners and the round of ritual
precautions. The generals in the old
days had tended to dismiss diviners
as a bunch of manipulative squeakers,
but they saw the First Exorcist as
something else; his profundity and
lucidity as state advisor impressed
them to a man, disconcerting many
and secretly frightening some. His
own colleagues had no choice but
to endure iron domination imposed
soon after his appointment. At this
point of his departure his power was
almost boundless and his reputation
as the foremost scholar in the country
unchallenged. He wondered how
long it would be before they officially
appointed his deputy to succeed him.

He knew now what he was after. The
vision had been sharpening itself as

he walked or even when he slept. There was nothing left to strive for but central power. Triumph when his word was paramount was gratifying but transitory, and it was invariably power confined to right or wrong, success or failure, respect or calumny; not life itself and death itself. And that was his rightful arena, to play king, pitting rival against rival, manoeuvring chaos to restore order or order to chaos, dispensing pain and loss of life with a free hand, the sole intermediary with divinity, in ultimate, untouchable control.

The role of master thinker, running king, country and empire, lured him now like the costliest drug, refined to perfection. He would empty a treasury to acquire it and kill with abandon to the same end, for its achievement promised unspeakable fulfilment and he knew it to be his ordained destiny.

And the stone, cleverly handled, would bring him all this.

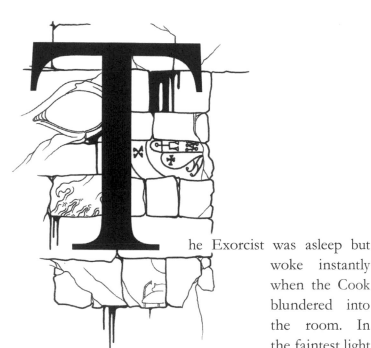

he Exorcist was asleep but woke instantly when the Cook blundered into the room. In the faintest light his companion seemed to have grown vastly in size; the Exorcist sat up and could not comprehend what was happening, but he stiffened himself in anticipation of difficulty. The Cook stood mutely looking down at him like an injured elephant, his great dark cloak wrapped around him. He had never seen the expression in the man's eyes before; in fact he had never witnessed such unfathomable appeal before. He stood up, and shook himself. He was ready.

The two men went outside the building and stood facing one another in the beginnings of the dawn. The Exorcist made a slight gesture and the Cook pulled aside his cloak and even his master recoiled in shock. A naked girl was spread-eagled around his thighs, impaled on the Cook's horse-like organ, which was still embedded in her body. She was clearly dead.

The Cook must have stood up and walked with his obscene frontage from whatever field or corner he had used to violate the girl. She had dark hair at their conjunction but hardly breasts and was perhaps fourteen. The Cook looked at the sky and gestured violently as if he wished to brush the girl from him as dirt from his clothes. The Exorcist came close. The Cook's organ was still fully erect, but she must have gone into a convulsive shock that left the muscles of her groin rigid and unyielding. In dying, impaled by the stake, her innermost muscles, powerful enough to expel a living child, had

combined to clench their violator in
startling revenge: he was unable by any
means to extricate himself from her
innards.

They must act quickly.

The Exorcist indicated that the Cook
should kneel down. He probed the
muscles. Perversely, the Cook was still
iron-hard; the onset of the fatal grasp
had preceded subsidence if, thought
the Exorcist, the thing ever did subside.
The only solution was to cut the girl's
body off. The Cook's great knife was
the perfect tool. With difficulty, he
tugged it from the folds at his hip and
proceeded to slice through the taut
tendons at the top of the girl's thighs,
then cutting and slicing until the
bloodied adornment fell to the ground.
There was a slight knick from the blade
on the Cook's organ but he just laughed
in his inaudible fashion and rubbed the
blood off the shaft.

Another body for disposal, then, and
no clear option. The only answer was
to return to the river that was a day
behind them and sink it in a sack with
a necklace of stones as dowry. They left
at once together on foot, the larger with
the burden, speaking to no one, in a

curious state of harmony. They walked
day and night until they caught up with
the caravan. Unspoken between them
lay their freshly sharpened kinship in
killing.

The lesson was not lost on the Exorcist,
however, that the needy Cook could
bring trouble for them both. They
would kill together whenever necessary
over the time to come, but no one
could ever connect a disappearance
with the taciturn, private traveller
and his great, unspeaking companion.
True, the Cook could never talk. True,
too, he was stronger than any man the
Exorcist had ever encountered and
would be loyal beyond death, but his
need for women might prove to be
more than a liability.

Thus mused the Exorcist, as he lay alert
on his cot in the caravanserai some days
later. The giant's physical urges had
not concerned him in any way in their
day-to-day life at the College, but they
were clearly not to be underestimated.
The prostrate companion beside him
now was replete and unconscious,
having eaten and drunk uninhibitedly.
Even now, the dreaming Cook's hand
rested on the bulge at his groin. The
Exorcist had no prurient interest, being

himself quite devoid of such urgings; if he had experienced them at all they were long beyond recall. But the Cook, over-endowed in any case by normal standards, had a third testicle, as he had discovered with fascination when the boy first came to him. The Exorcist had thought that the gland would atrophy or not grow to maturity, but that had not happened. The Cook was thus prodigiously virile; with curled locks instead of his shaved head, and a combed out beard he could be sculpted as a hero wrestling with a lion.

If it ever came to it, disposal of his companion would be no easy matter. He could never escape: the Cook would find him by a hundred unmistakable signs that would be unnoticed by anyone else. The Exorcist readied himself for sleep in the darkness. If he must kill the Cook in the end, it would not be through muscular prowess.

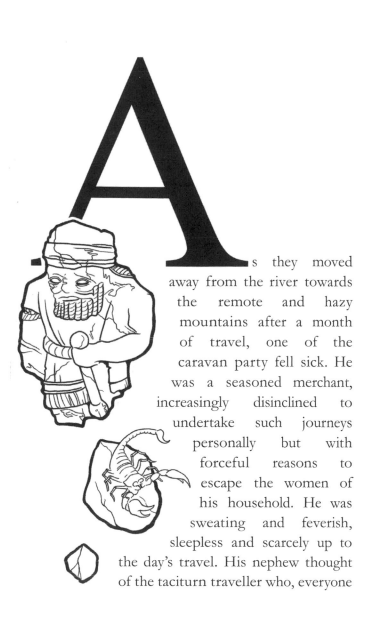

As they moved away from the river towards the remote and hazy mountains after a month of travel, one of the caravan party fell sick. He was a seasoned merchant, increasingly disinclined to undertake such journeys personally but with forceful reasons to escape the women of his household. He was sweating and feverish, sleepless and scarcely up to the day's travel. His nephew thought of the taciturn traveller who, everyone said, could read, and therefore must be some kind of healer. The Exorcist accepted the summons silently and appeared in the tent doorway with that look of authority that had earned him a private fortune at bedsides in the capital. No one present could see in the poor light the small familiar that crouched for a moment on his shoulder, come when summoned, its wings folded, its breath in his ear. The Exorcist saw at once that the man's sickness was nothing to be feared and would undoubtedly clear on its own in two days if left untreated. This was ideal. He stooped over his patient. Similar cases in the past, brought by his powerful magic to successful outcome, seemed to be flitting through his mind as he looked down with hooded eyes. Then he sat at the edge of the bed and lightly touched the man's temples with the tips of his fingers, gazing into the distance and saying nothing at all. At length he nodded. He took from his bag the purloined fragment of rock crystal and placed the point very gently in the middle of the man's forehead. The merchant lay as if paralysed. Then the Exorcist drew the point slowly over the man's profile and then over his neck and down the right side of his chest to the hip, the thigh, and down to the foot, pronouncing almost inaudibly a stream of unintelligible words. As the crystal worked its way to the tip of the big toe, the Exorcist plunged the crystal point into a small worked ball of clay. Finally he wrote some signs on it and strode wordlessly out of the room; the merchant's servant saw him hurl the small sphere far from the caravan track into the distant scrubland. From that moment, the sick man slept like a child, oblivious when carried to the cart, and, by evening, was fully recovered.

This achievement enhanced the Exorcist's status instantly; more than mere courtesy was directed towards him, and it became needful for him to imply graciously that, for inner reasons, he often needed solitude. Everyone felt that sickness on the trip was no longer to be feared, and the Cook found food and drink and conviviality wherever he turned.

* * *

The Exorcist knew himself on the verge of a new stage of history. That the oddly-shaped piece was the nose of a statue, broken off to bear its message, was an interpretation that might well be useful to present to the world but he knew it beyond doubt to be nonsense. That the signs contained a divine message was ineluctable. But he could not credit that a finished statue of carved, worked stone could be full of signs waiting to be deciphered. In the usual way of the world, protuberances on sculptures were only broken off in times of war, as conquerors rushed to defile sanctuaries and images. A nose of stone was no medium for important messages of huge import. The idea made no sense. But if the fragment were the broken-off lug of a stone vessel that just *looked* like a nose, then understanding could follow. Such a vessel, heavy and strong, could have been made in the east somewhere out of local material that, unbeknownst to the craftsman, contained the message. The vessel, loaded, say, with a costly aromatic or an exotic drug, would travel far from its place of origin to who knows where. The day would come when one lug that had borne half the weight would snap off, to reveal the message waiting inside for those who could understand it. At the pre-ordained moment the stone would crack, and, like a bell sounding a pure note, proclaim its message, setting wheels to turn, carrying it here and there until, at last, it reached the one person in all the kingdom who could be expected to read and act upon its wording.

This interpretation seemed far more credible. The question then arose, was this remarkable stone always full of writing, or had not some god seized the chance to send him a message, much as the god of the sun might write his message on a sheep's liver for the diviners to find? This last thought brought the whole matter into a familiar theatre. It was a *message*, then, from the gods, to *him*. This was a gratifying conclusion. At the same time, however, the Exorcist could not quite make himself believe that the vessel with its lug message could be unique.

More probable was it that, somewhere, stones full of writing were to be found, and that this one, on this occasion, had been used to call him. Perhaps in the untouched stone the wedge shapes that made up the signs were stored in neat rows – horizontals, verticals and diagonals – within the body of the stone itself, like palette colours for a wall painting. If he could find that source and control it, the power it would confer was literally dizzying to think of. He would be the only person standing within the whole of the World, ringed round with the un-crossable Bitter Sea, who could understand and profit from this new form of knowledge.

He thought back to his first deep study of the priest's stone. He had focused on it the most extreme percipience of which he was capable, scrutinising the unfolding facets of inscription under light sharpened through a vial of water, or trying the early morning sun for the sharpest shadows. Among the uncountable wedges within the stone were some that combined themselves into conventional and easily recognisable signs that any sceptical colleague,would have to acknowledge as intelligible. For the other, unknown signs, identities and meanings would have to be *invented*, wherever possible with the help of existing signs. Given time, he could arrange it. They would have to believe whatever he told them. That understanding had come to him in a dream, for example. Or that he had found additional deep messages. Any future interpretation that he might need to broadcast would be entirely his domain, for he had the stone itself and it was certain by now that no one on the face of the earth knew that it still existed.

By now, he could sense, the Dwarf had seen to it that both the Deputy and the Third Exorcist were dead. His College would be in chaos; teaching might go on, but high-level work would soon compel the king to bring in someone from outside, probably from Babylon, to support the intelligence services. All, with the exception of the newcomer, would be delighted when he returned.

And if he had found nothing on the excursion, so be it; he knew that he could still exploit the existing stone to lethal effect. To undermine the king, and sap his authority permanently. That king, who, like the other gaming pieces playing out on the great board before him, had scrabbled himself to put the stone into his waiting hands. By the time he was ready, the king would never protest that he had seen the stone before, or that he, the First Exorcist, had given him the very dust into which it had supposedly disintegrated. If, on the other hand, he were to discover further pieces, everything would follow much more easily. His so-called fellow savants would be dumbfounded, obliged to credit whatever he told them and fulfil whatever injunctions he thrust on them. It would mean an exquisite profundity of corruption, a gambler with doctored dice playing all for fools, laughing up his expensively embroidered but discreetly closed-up sleeves.

The Exorcist was discomfited only by the idea of the unsuspected *cave*, knowledge of whose existence he had forced from the skull. It gaped now blackly in his imagination. The account was not to be dismissed; he had heard the truth as his victim had known it and been forced to tell it. One musician, who had acquired the stone as one oddment among others from some other person, with a cave *full of writing* in the background. The words ran round and round in his mind. It was one thing to track down an individual, a market stall, an old exchange, but quite another to identify a cave. A cave across the mountains laden with wedge-shaped signs of power would not suit him at all. Taking pieces home might be feasible, but leaving the rest for someone else to discover would not do for his plan at all; he might have to block it up, or even destroy it. That cave, he reflected, stumbling suddenly on a sharp rock that seemed to have cut his foot rather deeply, represented danger.

He thought again about the long-haired, wandering musician. Of all itinerants he should be findable. So far, so good. He knew something about music, and could play passably on a lute himself. That could be a good way to establish… *friendship*. He grinned to himself.

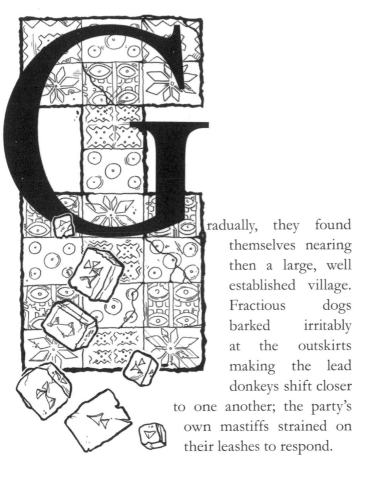

radually, they found themselves nearing then a large, well established village. Fractious dogs barked irritably at the outskirts making the lead donkeys shift closer to one another; the party's own mastiffs strained on their leashes to respond.

The caravan leader, travel-worn, was tense in the fading light as always when people approached, but they were friendly enough with offers of milk or meat. They spoke a northern dialect that the caravan people seemed to know but it was not a tongue that the Exorcist had met before. There was a place with beer and several of the men left their women to their own devices and walked off between the houses, the Cook with them. The Exorcist lay under the expanse of the sky, his eye running over the familiar paths, noting locations, filled briefly with a yearn for the days with the old sky records, plaiting the strands together into one meaningful, moving canopy, reading the complex interplays with their warnings of good or dread. Then he had known tranquillity.

Before the fit had come upon him.

And the stone.

No one looked up when he entered the low chamber. There were oil lamps flaring on the walls, and low divans with men sprawled around. Some were concentrating on a board game that had been embroidered onto a piece of carpet. There were excited cries to accompany the throws, and shouts as the pieces played out their contest. The

Cook was not to be seen; the Exorcist sat cross-legged on a low bench near the door observing, unnoticed, all that was going on. In the opposite corner in poor light two men were intent on some gambling game; a burly northerner with few teeth was drinking freely and periodically guessing throws, each time unsuccessfully. After a while he stood up, red-faced, and in his own patois accused the other of cheating. The other man, older but fitter looking, ignored him until the brawler was thrown out. The Cook came in then, and with the slightest of head movements he told him to drink with the gambler.

Once a good deal more had gone down the man's throat the Exorcist climbed to his feet and went over to the two men as if on impulse, sat, and took some beer himself. The stranger, having escaped the consequences of his trickery, grew suddenly expansive. He was a typical person of the road, grubby, dressed in a variety of wrappings, and obviously flexible in ways of earning a living. Before long, he was boasting that he had magic dice, unique dice that never betrayed him so that he always won. The Exorcist was interested, for everything unusual caught his attention. The gambler would not, however, surrender them for inspection by any means. The Exorcist called for more beer, and led the traveller to talk of other things. After a while, as he knew would happen, the man returned to the subject himself. He had six magic dice, he said, although he only used three at a time. They had come from his father. They were unlike any other dice in the world for they were made not of bone but *stone*.

"Not possible," said the Exorcist knowingly. "No one could make stone dice."

"Stone they are. Shining. Like from the stars. And the numbers..." mumbled the other.

The Exorcist waited. The Cook yawned, and finished his beer, looking round.

"No one can understand them. They are written…"

The Exorcist remarked in a bored tone that he had seen many dice in his time and the numbers were always little holes. The gambler reached under his jacket and after a struggle pulled out one of the dice. He held out his hand with it lying on the open palm. The

Exorcist felt his heart lurch and his very brain reel. It was a perfectly formed cube of some bright, shiny stone that looked like a meteorite. The numbers in the middle of each face were not in any way conventional dots. They stuck out proud of the surface.

Each of the numbers was made up of writing wedges.

This, too, was no work of man. Again the Exorcist felt his mind swivel on the cusp of madness. This object, in the hands of this peasant, was also from the gods. It had to be. It was the same story. No man could make such a thing. He poured more beer. This, then, was also a sign to him. Once from a king, once from the trough. A thing of indisputably heavenly origin. Writing in stone.

He said nothing. They drank deep together.

"My father found them," said the gambler later. "I have six. From him. He said they were for me."

"Do you know," asked the Exorcist casually, "where your father found them?"

"There was a mountain in the East. He went there. He said there was a stream, shining in the sunshine, that poured in a crooked line down the side of the mountain. He was thirsty, but when he got close he saw that it was not water, but dice like these, thousands of them, pouring out of a crack in the mountain and running down, one over another, gleaming as if they were alive. He put in his hands and held onto six. He is dead. Now I have them."

He would not produce the others, and in his fumbling he dropped the die onto the floor. Instantly the Exorcist was in a crouch, his vulture's eyes spotting one shiny corner of the little cube amid the rubbish. He picked it up carefully and examined it minutely, with the slightest delay before handing it to its owner. The two of them got him really drunk then, and the Exorcist was careful to ensure that his broad and long-unwashed sash got left behind when he finally stumbled off to sleep. The minute he was gone the Exorcist knew what to do.

Outside, moving together in silence, they went to the fiercest of the great caravan mastiffs. It was sleeping, and they had time to slip the sash over its head and round its neck before it fully awoke. The Cook stunned it with a blow to the head and then squeezed the noose to the point of near asphyxiation. At the same time the Exorcist cut the dog in several places round the groin until its struggles were uncontrollable. Then the Cook knocked it out completely. They wiped the pungent cloth back and forth across its muzzle and left a torn fragment of it in the dog's mouth.

It was a simple matter in the darkness to drop the sash where its owner would automatically put it on the next morning.

While people were packing up kit and seeing to the donkeys at first light there came the noise of a violent altercation and hysterical barking. The Exorcist stepped out in concern. Many people were standing around. The gambler with whom they had been drinking lay just outside the door with his throat torn out. The great hound, blood at its jowls, was the embodiment of savagery. The Exorcist knelt gravely as if to see what could be done for his patient, and, with fluent dexterity and quite unnoticed, located the dice pouch under the man's tunic and had it out and hidden within seconds. The mastiff was still dangerous. It had licked its own wounds, invisible under its fur, but it was only with the caressing touch and the whispered words of the Exorcist when he stooped by the frantic animal that its rage came to subside, and it wandered off. No one thought of punishing the dog; he was there to kill intruders. The dead gambler must have been trying to steal from them and was nothing to cry over. At length, the caravan reassembled itself and they departed.

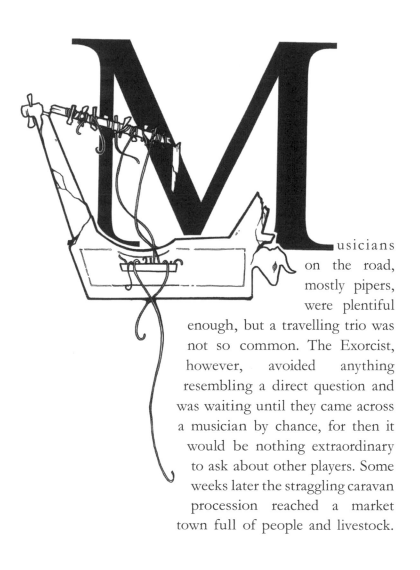

usicians
on the road,
mostly pipers,
were plentiful
enough, but a travelling trio was
not so common. The Exorcist,
however, avoided anything
resembling a direct question and
was waiting until they came across
a musician by chance, for then it
would be nothing extraordinary
to ask about other players. Some
weeks later the straggling caravan
procession reached a market
town full of people and livestock.

There were endless carts on the road, sluggish or inefficient. The merchants were relieved; they would stay for a week or more.

The Cook needed some fun. In his usual economic way the Exorcist indicated that if there were musicians in the town he wanted to know, but that he should proceed carefully. The Cook had grinned in understanding and disappeared shortly thereafter.

The Exorcist was walking alone, very early the following morning, isolated and thoughtful. He had disposed of the gambler's bag, and kept the dice wrapped in a finger of silk, carefully stowed away. Now he took them out again, hunting for their internal system. The six glittering jewels had quickly come to obsess his mind, for, just as with the stone, there could only be the one explanation – that they had come from the gods to him. The wedge numbers, like the signs in the stone, defied understanding. They bulged out of the stone cubes as if trying to escape, clusters of ones and tens and other wedge-shaped forms that altogether he thought must belong to some unknown and immensely ancient counting system. Their shapes corresponded to none of the dice options of one to six, where opposite faces would add up to seven. What numbers he could understand were far too big for dice scores, but the combinations of wedges were just as unintelligible as the signs in the stone. He had the idea that perhaps the number of wedges made up the totals, but that did not work either. He thought he could develop a private divination technique in which the thirty-six faces, once systematised, could be relied on for a yes or no answer. He would need to find clay and draw out a list of all the numbers to see what they suggested. They could bolster his future explanations of the stone text, for one thing. And somehow, he thought, the magic dice might help him identify the cave mountain, when the time came.

* * *

The Exorcist saw the long-haired musician, who was very tall but no young man, actually carrying his instrument in the market, and knew at once that this was the supplier of the stone to the Healer. He followed him through the throng unobserved, his cloak round the lower part of his face, the Cook striding many paces behind him. He wanted for now only to discover where the man was staying. The Exorcist was charged with a fine, trembling excitement, for the gods had led him, step by laborious step, to locate the one human being within the borders of the whole world whom he needed to meet. Given what was at stake, the only thing to do was to abduct him and get all the answers out of him. They discovered he had a room in one of the many sprawling lodging houses. After dark, he stood outside the unshuttered window with the Cook. The musician, they could see, lay inside the room with a girl. The Cook climbed straight into the room with incredible agility, lifted the man right off the bed and pushed him, three-quarters asleep, out into the street. There, he was instantly gagged by the Exorcist, and quickly tied so that he could not struggle. They half carried the figure between them down to the river and onto a partly-loaded raft that they had picked out before. Within moments, the Cook had untied the craft and poled it out into mid-stream, to be carried well away from the town by the current. They had him on his back. The Cook held him tightly in position by his hair and the Exorcist knelt on his chest. He produced the stone and held it in front of his eyes under the paleness of the moon.

"Do you know this stone?"

The man widened his eyes and, eventually, nodded.

"Where did you get it?"

The musician, still gagged, struggled to speak. The Exorcist cut off the gag and kept the knife visible.

"I got it when I was a boy."

"Where from?"

The man looked at him.

"Why do you want to know?"

The Exorcist nodded and the Cook wrenched out a large clump of his hair by the roots.

"Tell me – instantly – where you got it."

The musician screamed.

"Scream if you will. There is no one on the water to hear. Now listen carefully. You will tell me what I want to know at once or we will kill you with pain. We know how to do that. We have done it many times. It will be all night before you are actually dead. First, some fingers… No more melodies, no more voice… You understand?"

The fanatical, lethal violence within the Exorcist was writhing now like a serpent tied in a sack. The musician lay still, suddenly. He had seen in his assailant the personification of mortal danger.

"I got it from an old man. He had many unusual pieces. But only one stone like that. He gave it to me for my good fortune."

The phrase rang out strangely; both men knew the irony of it simultaneously.

"Where did he get it?"

"I remember just what he told me. He said it came from a cave in a mountain. In the north. He found the cave himself. It had stone writing on the walls and he found one broken piece of the stone there and brought it away."

"Where was the mountain?"

"I know only the north. Far from here. Far from everywhere."

The Exorcist very deliberately lifted the knife.

"I know no more. Except…"

"Yes?"

"He said the mountain top looked like a mountaineer's felt headgear; the tip pointed to one side."

"Have you ever seen another piece?"

"Never. It is all in that cave."

"Have you told anyone else about it?"

"No one ever, but that healer. He took it from me. Gave me some rubbish in return. My luck went with it."

"That it did."

As one man they rolled him over the edge of the raft into the river and Cook went in after him to drown him.

As they marched together, the two of them, across the stretch of wooded terrain, the great Cook's strength seemed inexhaustible, even when food came but infrequently.

One night, as they slept under their cloaks, the Exorcist dreamed restlessly of a giant toothed fish that flapped vengefully from the water with a baleful eye that promised ill. The dream, short but disturbing, came twice again. As they tramped forwards the next day, he mused over its meaning, for it was impossible that it could be empty of significance, but for once was unable to read for certain what that dream boded for them.

They walked on steadily for days. Ahead, at length, were the foothills of the mountains that lay ahead of them. Far off a succession of remote peaks retreated into the haze. How was he to identify the mountain with his cave? The Exorcist carried the stone in his hand waiting for a sign, the dice in their sheath over his heart. And then, wordless with shock, he glimpsed for a moment a misty profile that matched the description; the bent jester's cap was unmistakable.

He stopped abruptly, his heart beating so erratically that he felt giddy. The Cook read his master's exhilaration at once, but for him food was more urgent. First brushwood and fallen timber to make a fire, then he vanished in pursuit of game. The Exorcist sat upright on the thick, unfamiliar ferns beneath the tree-trunks, gazing at the mountain ahead wherein the stone cave was to be found. The strange months of zigzag travel across desert and highland had at last focused on this, their goal. There were thin, golden filaments in the light that seemed to radiate down from the mountain and beckon to him. He breathed slowly in the diluted, windless air, harnessing his strength, bracing his muscles for what lay ahead. He was thin in body but the energy burned undiminished within him; to walk on, or climb steadily upwards for a month would not have troubled him; like a hunting dog bewitched by some scent, he could track the cave of writings now with his eyes closed.

Then there was a smell of bitter wood smoke; he saw the great back of the Cook bent over smouldering logs, several small carcasses run through with a sticks propped already in the smoke; the man could generate a crucial domesticity in the very wilderness.

The Cook brought him cold river water in his drinking cup and a great wedge of steaming, greasy fish. The flesh was hot under his fingers and the bones were like needles; some worth keeping and drying; they would have a hundred uses later. He could not remember so large a fish in the rivers at home; the monster must have grazed, unrivalled and complacent among the rushes, for years, before the Cook, cunning in the ways of life, could take it from the shallows with his hands. It was long after he had eaten his fill, chilled and unmoving in the swirling dusk, that he remembered the recurring message-dream. He sat up violently.

The Cook lay on his back by the edge of the river, one of his feet in the embers. His face was convulsed; he must have been choking and vomiting with his hands at his throat for a long time before the great fish bone that stilled his massive chest killed him. Kneeling by him in the night air, the Exorcist touched his neck, knowing there would be no pulse more from that explosive life. Unable to cry out for the rescue that he could so easily have brought him, his wordless and most stalwart companion would remain silent forever.

The Exorcist sat by the corpse until first light with his hand resting on the Cook's great heart. There was no possibility of burial; there was no tool, and the physical labour in any case would be beyond him. It struck him that the dismemberment and digestion of his own body by passing carnivores would probably amuse the Cook if he were watching; it was, he would think, only just.

The Exorcist knew he would never find a replacement for his loyal giant. So be it. There was no counting the years that he had been followed by strength and devotion. His thoughts lingered only briefly on his new predicament; ahead the cave awaited him, and he would take his chances with the rest. Nothing could come to harm him. He was impervious to interference or interruption. He would travel on now, following his destiny. The return would mean new paths or waterways, back down to the far flat lands, guided by the fabric of the stars, buoyant with knowledge.

But alone.

he Exorcist stood at the very entrance to the cave, shading his eyes, looking outwards. He had climbed mechanically from the foothills to the first slopes and then onward and upward as if his route was rehearsed. The only cave of any size was turned away from the narrow path, laid into a great wall of rock that leaned out over a ravine, and he had to climb up carefully without the Cook's burly support to reach the opening. The cave mouth gaped blackly; light from outside fell just at the opening and he waited until his eyes were no longer blind.

He had been carrying several burnt sticks from their last fire, easy enough to re-kindle. He held the spindly light aloft and stepped carefully across the broken floor into the body of the cave. It was roughly square, infinitely larger and higher than could have been imagined from outside; as his eyes adjusted he grasped its immensity. A further opening, like a city gate, led out from the left hand side of the chamber into deeper darkness beyond.

From his vantage point the Exorcist made out that the far back wall of the cave had a great rift running across it, as if the living rock had been repeatedly slashed with a sharp weapon. He found himself irresistibly drawn towards it, stepping slowly and nursing his torch until he found himself directly facing the gashed face of the stone. It was if some giant being had ravaged the face of the stone with unimaginable claws, ripping it open and displaying its innards. In the flickering uncertainty of the briefly flaring wood, the broken surface danced before his eyes, but as he gazed he came to see what he knew would be there: the inner facets and folds revealed within the stone were crammed with thousands upon thousands of perfectly shaped cuneiform signs.

The Exorcist's mind, cold and steady, wavered again at the enormity. For, as he examined the wounds in the stone, walking from left to right and tracing the depth of the sharp ridges with his fingertips, he came to realize that the whole rock of the cave walls must be full of wedges. Wherever it was opened by a reader pursuing knowledge or sovereignty the inside would show impressions of all sizes, combined together as if fallen from the surface of a tablet and swept together in a heap. Wherever he looked, there were message wedges that receded beyond capture, folded under other wedges, piled on top of others into chaos and madness. Not even the quarry teams with their prisoners-of-war and rhythmic work songs could tackle this, no fleet of rafts could manoeuvre a whole cave down the river to the capital and into his safekeeping, and if the chisellers tried to take it in portions the inscriptions inside would be fatally disturbed. A lump, like the priest's stone, would be all that he could take, even if he could break it off with nothing more than his hands.

And then, gradually, far deeper understanding began to dawn in his mind. There was no volcano of wisdom here that he could ever harness for his own purposes as he had assumed. He grasped then that the opening in the stone was like a cut-into pomegranate with its compacted waiting seeds; the whole mountain and the mountains behind it, must be full of wedges too. And eventually he came to the deepest truth, that this was where the gods stored what they needed for writing, layers and layers of waiting signs, ready for use to give force and vitality to their plans and decisions. So the mountains were their medium, as clay from the river was his, but while man had to write each sign, stroke by stroke, the gods were supplied with infinite, perfect signs ready for use: they would take what they needed. Perhaps they simply blew the wedges and signs out of the stone onto their own tablets, so that, as they spoke aloud, the signs formed themselves into messages, or records, that would last forever.

And what could he possibly do, halfway across the world and alone, a single intruder in the gods' private scriptorium? He could take nothing away, no fragment could be of use because it took a god to make a message out of the timeless signs and every single sign belonged here.

The Exorcist turned slowly on his heel. He had become aware that he had stepped where no human had preceded him, and that, despite all his learning, he had seen what no man should see. His journey had been vanity, his ideas all mortal frailty, his deeds, too, were hidden from none and recorded for perpetuity. There would be no harvest, no yielded fruit at all, such as he had promised the king.

And then, as he stood there in dawning awareness of what lay before him, he heard a noise.

A final wave of understanding swept over him.

The cave of the gods had a guardian.

There were always guardians. At the cosmic gates that kept the universe in place. The gates where the sun passed through in timeless circles; always guarded. And he, without defences and in unflinching arrogance, had simply left unconsidered that the gods would never leave their mountain message stronghold undefended. He thought of spells, but they were all against evil, or for evil. He thought of prayers, but what could he ask for? The gods were watching him and he could have done no more to offend them if that had been his sole intention. And now, because of him, their Watchman was roused.

The Exorcist, drained of power and ambition, found himself incapable of movement. He knew he had stopped breathing. The light of his torch had burned out unnoticed; his eyes strained in the dark, part of his violently bruised mind still curious. Behind him, in the world that he had now left, he heard the sound of sudden and violent heavy rain; there was a remote tumble of thunder from beyond the mountain range, a ripple of resentful outcry.

And then, from in front of him, there was a second noise, a shuffling sound. It came from the great doorway in the corner, and he realised that this must be its home; it didn't live in the Cave with the signs, but beyond, in the blackness, through the great opening. He sensed rather than saw movement, then a brilliant flash of lightning poured in and illumined the great arched temple of the cave and he saw for himself what stood in front of him. A vast, towering reptile, its shape imprinted on his mind as the blackness reshaped itself.

It was the kind of deadly reptile that certain priests he knew kept chained in temples, captured in the countryside after snatching a goat or a child. Some said the stench of their breath killed at once, others that the shock and terror were enough. They were rabidly carnivorous, with nightmare teeth to match.

The gods, then, had such a monitor of their own, seemingly carved out of stone, but of staggering, unimaginable size. Its eyes were made up of several sections, he noted, dead and undiscriminating. It would not see in him a wedge reader, come in homage from the end of the earth to bow at the feet of the gods' librarian. It would know exactly what he was, and what it had to do.

He heard it move again.

The dragon was like him. Cold ran its heart, sluggish its blood; its unused ability to outrun a sandstorm was evident in its great, unmoving haunches; the back legs splayed like a whore; its front upright in bestial arrogance; a great tail snaked back into the doorway. He thought fleetingly of all the dragons of which he had read, the composite beasts that strode beside the gods, half-snake, half-legged, with breath that meant death, claws dripping gall, crushers of stone, rippers of flesh. The old dragon words ran in his mind: *I know what you are, he thought; I know what you are. I have seen what no man has seen since before the Flood.* When the lightning came again his scholar's mind looked for the claws, hooked and ridged like those of an eagle, the huge curved nails resting neatly on the floor. The claws were perfectly sculpted to slash open a living being, and it came to him that it must be one of the Guardian's duties, to slash open the rock when new signs were needed.

It was then that the great stone lizard coughed.

Its breath was not foul, but musty and cold, like the cellars under the palace where they had interrogated the Elamite spies. He saw then that the great reptile was unimaginably old, and that it must have been at its post here since the beginning of time. Any response would be slow; perhaps, if he moved quickly…

But, as he stood irresolute before it, he saw the stone eyes suddenly flicker into living colour, greenish-yellow and bloodshot; the eyes swivelled around, and looked at him. Then lightning ran in a flickering trail down its body to the end of its tail, and he saw the stone of the torso and legs become leathery, green skin and the head jutting into tense alertness, its mouth slightly open. There was an abominable stench of decay around him as the vast, unimaginable creature breathed.

As he felt his senses and his mind slide away forever, the Exorcist saw, clear in the darkness, the face of his sister; then the Guardian sliced him to pieces with a contemptuous flick of its waiting claw.

This narrative takes place in the world of Ancient Mesopotamia, Assyria to the north and Babylonia to the south, of what is today the country of Iraq. The very process of writing began in this part of the world. The script is known as cuneiform, and was written by impressing clay tablets with a writing-stick that left wedge-shaped impressions, so each individual sign was formed of special arrangements of wedges.

These clay documents survive in their tens of thousands, so today Assyriologists know a great deal about the daily life of the ancient Mesopotamians, including politics and history, administration and economics, literature and grammar, astronomy and astrology, not to mention fortune-telling, medicine and magic against demons.

Cuneiform writing can be an outlet for calligraphic pride or just informal and untidy. Customised niches in the Great Library of Assyria at Nineveh housed immaculate documents in the most readable possible hand. Its founder, King Assurbanipal (668–c.627 BC), anticipating the library at Alexandria, sought to bring the whole of inherited knowledge under one roof. He had been trained as a priest, could argue with the most learned in the land, and was surely never happier than when presented with some new, venerable manuscript.

Real cuneiform writing

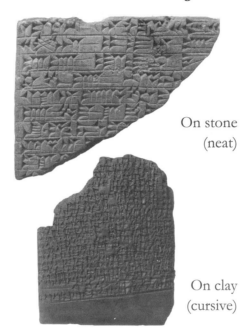

On stone
(neat)

On clay
(cursive)

The mysterious stone inscription with cuneiform signs that forms the centrepiece of this book is real. It is probably a lug from the side of a large vessel that sheared off where it sustained the maximum strain. The stone of which it was made, limestone or marble, has the curious characteristic that, when fractured, the result is a cracked face made up completely of cuneiform (i.e. wedge) shapes. It thus resembles the historic cuneiform script of ancient Mesopotamia to a quite startling degree.

The stone "dice" with "cuneiform numbers" are equally real and entirely natural. The material is iron pyrites, sometimes known as "fool's gold". By some freak of geology this stone is often found in small finished cubes, as exact in proportion as most commercially made dice. In certain specimens one or more faces have a centrally-placed wedge-shaped protrusion highly evocative of the writing of numbers in cuneiform script. In countless examples from Iran seen by the author all six faces have such "numbers" placed right in the centre.

This story concerns the intellectual mayhem that would have resulted if this unique "cuneiform" stone had appeared in Nineveh, the Assyrian capital, during its heyday in the seventh century BC. No one would be able to read it. It could only have come from the gods.

The narrative imagines the impact on a highly placed royal diviner and exorcist, a brilliant and successful scholar who is compelled to act swiftly, but with quite unseen consequences.

The narrative is thus a What-would-have-happened? conceit, but derives from the author's conviction that human nature in all its facets remains unchanged throughout time, and that psychopaths will have existed in ancient Mesopotamia (without detectives or clues) as they do now. The author has spent his life among cuneiform inscriptions, and has tried in writing this narrative to reflect something of the Mesopotamian view of things visible and invisible, and show how the Assyrians and Babylonians came to terms with the world around them. Nothing that happens contradicts the evidence of ancient documents. The underlying struggle, however, while anchored in the landscape of ancient Iraq, does not stop there, for conflict between the forces of light and dark and the forces recruited to control them will never disappear from the human stage.

The wedges embedded in the stone even include real cuneiform signs that would be read at sight by an Assyrian, side by side with numberless arrangements that would remain unintelligible forever.

That geology can furnish its own cuneiform writing and numbers provokes reflection. Ephemeral cloud formations or patterns in the sand can sometimes be "read" in one or other script, and the curious could no doubt assemble a compelling dossier of such phenomena, inhibited only by the realisation that the English language apparently contains no word for "writing imitated by nature".

In view of *pareidolia* and other nouns already in the dictionary, we propose the freshly-coined word *paragraff*.